# Morpho Amathonte

## Victoria Arnette & Dennis Arnette

Morpho Amathonte
Copyright © 2024 by Victoria Arnette & Dennis Arnette.
All rights reserved.

This is a work of fiction. Names, characters, places and incidents are products of the author's imagination or are used fictitiously and should not be construed as real. Any resemblance to actual events, locales, organizations or persons, living or dead, is entirely coincidental.

No part of this book may be used or reproduced in any manner whatsoever without written permission, except in the case of brief quotations embodied in critical articles and reviews. For more information, e-mail all inquiries to info@mindstirmedia.com.

Published by MindStir Media, LLC
45 Lafayette Rd | Suite 181| North Hampton, NH 03862 | USA
1.800.767.0531 | www.mindstirmedia.com

Printed in the United States of America.
ISBN-Paperback: 978-1-961532-45-8
ISBN-Hardcover: 978-1-963844-52-8

# Table of Contents

Chapter 1: The Celestials . . . . . . . . . . . . 23
Chapter 2: The Stellar Sentinel *Synus* . . . . . . . . 33
Chapter 3: The Guardians . . . . . . . . . . . 39
Chapter 4: The Arrival . . . . . . . . . . . . 50
Chapter 5: Grayville . . . . . . . . . . . . . 53
Chapter 6: The Canvas . . . . . . . . . . . . 56
Chapter 7: Delirium Tremens . . . . . . . . . . 64
Chapter 8: Home Sweet Home . . . . . . . . . 71
Chapter 9: The Artist . . . . . . . . . . . . 80
Chapter 10: The Antiqua Bibliotheca . . . . . . . 83
Chapter 11: The Shmygs . . . . . . . . . . . 90
Chapter 12: The Mill . . . . . . . . . . . . . 97
Chapter 13: The Miner . . . . . . . . . . . 101
Chapter 14: Shmygus Superiors . . . . . . . . 105
Chapter 15: The Underground . . . . . . . . 109
Chapter 16: Tiberius . . . . . . . . . . . . 116
Chapter 17: The Covert Operation . . . . . . . 121
Chapter 18: The Manipulator . . . . . . . . . 124
Chapter 19: Chubata . . . . . . . . . . . . 127
Chapter 20: The Cat Race . . . . . . . . . . 133
Chapter 21: The Secret Recipe . . . . . . . . . 137
Chapter 22: The MTech 5000 . . . . . . . . . 142

Chapter 23: The Theory of Chaos
& Incredible Coincidences . . . . . . . . . . . . . . . *151*
Chapter 24: Pentoball. . . . . . . . . . . . . . . . . . *155*
Chapter 25: The Psychotherapist . . . . . . . . . *161*
Chapter 26: Gestalt. . . . . . . . . . . . . . . . . . . . *167*
Chapter 27: Psycho-Surfing . . . . . . . . . . . . . *185*
Chapter 28: A Nervous Breakdown . . . . . . . . *189*
Chapter 29: The Secret Police . . . . . . . . . . . *194*
Chapter 30: The Resort. . . . . . . . . . . . . . . . . *198*
Chapter 31: Hibernation . . . . . . . . . . . . . . . *201*
Chapter 32: The Father. . . . . . . . . . . . . . . . . *203*
Chapter 33: The Experiment . . . . . . . . . . . . *207*
Chapter 34: The Hangover . . . . . . . . . . . . . . *215*
Chapter 35: A Dream Within A Dream . . . . . *219*
Chapter 36: The Diagnosis . . . . . . . . . . . . . . *236*
Chapter 37: The Hospital. . . . . . . . . . . . . . . *240*
Chapter 38: The Insight . . . . . . . . . . . . . . . . *246*
Chapter 39: The Rainbow. . . . . . . . . . . . . . . *251*
Chapter 40: The Pollination . . . . . . . . . . . . . *254*
Chapter 41: What A Wonderful World . . . . . *263*
Chapter 42: Sky . . . . . . . . . . . . . . . . . . . . . . *272*

Dear Reader,

Thank you for your support. We are delighted that *Morpho Amathonte*, our debut book, is now in your hands. We hope your journey through its fantasy world proves to be enchanting.

This story is unique, carrying a heartfelt wish from us to you. We invite you to explore our story with an open heart and a receptive mind, confident that you will find its message inspiring.

We are deeply grateful to our parents for their unconditional love and support—we love you dearly!

Warmest regards,
Dennis & Victoria

Dennis and Victoria Arnette, siblings who reside in a mountainous region of the United States, have cherished outdoor activities and nature play since their youth. Their childhood, marked by a joyful environment and a close circle of friends, was filled with imaginative games where they envisioned themselves as kings, queens, knights, and robbers. They climbed trees, walls, and mountains, embracing every climbable challenge they encountered. Their adventures were further enriched by various trips with their parents. These experiences during their formative years naturally sculpted them into fun-loving, hardworking, and creative individuals, with vibrant imaginations.

Dennis and Victoria, while not professional writers, have always harbored the ambition to collaborate on a writing project. From an early age, they were inspired by the fairy tales of the Brothers Grimm. Their favorite childhood moments were spent in the evenings, listening to their parents read classic stories like "The Bremen Town Musicians," "Snow White," "Little Red Riding Hood," and "Cinderella" before bedtime. This early exposure fueled their longstanding aspiration to craft a fairy tale or a fictional story aimed at an adult audience.

During the stressful period of the pandemic, they embarked on a lighthearted project to distract themselves and bring laughter to their family. They soon realized that this project had far greater potential than initially expected. They dedicated themselves to creating this beautiful book, and sincerely hope you enjoy reading it as much as they enjoyed writing it.

The name *Morpho amathonte* refers to a butterfly species known for its striking, iridescent blue wings. Native to the rainforests of Central and South America, these butterflies captivate both amateur enthusiasts and professional researchers with their unique light-reflecting properties. Universally admired for their beauty, *Morpho amathonte* butterflies have been extensively studied.

*Morpho Amathonte* is also the title of our captivating fictional tale, featuring otherworldly guardians battling malevolent creatures that manipulate the human mind. These guardians are on a quest to save Earth, embarking on an adventure-filled journey that explores the eternal struggle between good and evil, reflecting aspects of human nature. The fate of the guardians is intertwined with your journey through the book, a journey we hope will be joyful and memorable.

The front cover of our book showcases a stunning, magical butterfly woman, while the back cover features an equally mesmerizing butterfly man. Their gazes, filled with deep affection and passion, underscore a central theme of the book: life without love is meaningless. We extend our wishes of light and kindness to all our readers.

Every illustration within these pages springs from the imaginative minds of Victoria and Dennis Arnette, showcasing their creative prowess. These illustrations, along with the ideas they bring to life, are exclusively theirs—crafted, owned, and imbued with a distinct flair.

# Chapter 1

# The Celestials

*Bound by planetary thoughts, our minds may tether,*
*Yet urge we must, to shatter these chains forever.*

*When faith dwindles, conjure it from the void's embrace,*
*For space itself is a canvas of human curiosity and grace.*

*In the absence of heroes, step forth, become the light,*
*For fortune smiles upon the bold, those who ignite the night.*

*Audacious souls first carve the path, through the unknown they sail.*
*As eternal dreamers, these heroes dance on the sky's endless trail.*

*The Chief Guardian's Logbook:*
*Space Odyssey Chronicles*

Lea made sure to rest before exhaustion set in. She felt as if the stars had aligned just for her when she awoke with some time to spare before her duty shift started. Seizing the moment, she decided to enjoy a leisurely stroll.

As Lea walked along the passageway, her path was illuminated by the radiant sunrise. She basked in the joyous warmth of the sun, complemented by the gentle caress of a cool breeze. The corridors of the Stellar Sentinel spacecraft were transformed into vibrant gardens, showcasing a stunning array of flowers and plants from various planets. Each bloom and leaf contributed to the tapestry of beauty and serenity that enveloped her.

The vibrant turquoise light of the passageway illuminated Lea's eyes, which mirrored the vivid colors around her. A mere glance at Lea would reveal her origins from the distant planet Septarion. Septarioneons were distinguished by their striking eyes: blue butterfly irises dotted with gold around the pupils, set against fluffy black eyelashes and golden eyebrows that created a stark contrast with their pale skin. Their faces bore intricate golden patterns and lines, each a unique birthmark that not only resembled a map of Septarion but also enhanced their enchanting allure. Although Septarioneons shared a human-like form, they were taller and leaner, presenting a graceful deviation from the typical human silhouette. One very important fact about Septarioneons is that

they could transform into anything, that's why their bodies were extremely flexible.

Septarioneons were renowned for their high intelligence and values of honesty, justice, and reasonableness. These virtues were deeply ingrained in their beings, forming an intrinsic part of their existence. Lea was a paragon of Septarioneon ideals; her unwavering adherence to these values played a pivotal role in her appointment as chief guardian.

Becoming the chief guardian required rigorous trials that tested mental and character strength, with a focus on candidates' abilities to manage emergencies through psycho-behavioral assessments. These assessments evaluated their mental resilience, crisis management skills, and behavior under duress. Lea's remarkable qualifying score of 99.9% catapulted her into the elite ranks of the galaxy's most esteemed guardians, highlighting her exceptional intelligence, professional skill, and ethical integrity. This score was more than just a number; it was a testament to her extraordinary qualities that distinguished her in the vast expanse of the Morpho Amathonte galaxy.

Tasked with leading daring missions to safeguard the galaxy, the Central Galactic Commission recruited the finest and brightest for service aboard the Stellar Sentinel spacecraft. The guardians aboard the fleet of one thousand Stellar Sentinel spacecraft, cruising through the Morpho Amathonte galaxy to support a range of space endeavors, emerged as the heroes of these missions.

Brave adventurers from every corner of the vast Morpho Amathonte galaxy stepped forward, eager to join the elite crew of the Stellar Sentinel spacecraft. These positions demanded not just exceptional skills but also represented the highest honor for those chosen to lead missions and courageously venture into space. Securing these prestigious roles involved overcoming numerous challenging tests, each designed to assess the candidates' readiness for the unpredictable journeys of space. As applicants competed for a spot aboard the spacecraft, they underwent a series of rigorous assessments, preparing them to navigate the mysteries of the galaxy with bravery and zeal.

The Morpho Amathonte galaxy harbored a unique mystery: every action and its subsequent ripples were governed by the immutable laws of nature, intertwined with the whimsical Butterfly Effect, which heightened the unpredictability of each event. This synergy achieved a near-perfect accuracy rate of 99.9%. However, the elusive 0.1% uncertainty introduced by the Butterfly Effect served as a wildcard, turning absolute predictability into a galaxy-wide game of cosmic roulette. Thus, despite strict adherence to natural laws, the dream of achieving perfect 100% accuracy in every action and its consequences remained just that—a dream, due to the unpredictability of the Butterfly Effect.

This sliver of unpredictability ensured that the highest attainable score in any galaxy-wide evaluation was 99.9%. Reaching this pinnacle of performance was a formidable task, particularly for those competing for spots aboard the elite Stellar Sentinel spacecraft. The challenge was amplified by the masses of hopefuls from every corner of the galaxy, each vying to secure their place among the stars.

Amidst the star-strewn expanse of the Morpho Amathonte galaxy, an armada of a thousand Stellar Sentinel spacecraft wove through the cosmos, serving as defenders of peace and beacons of liberty. With every pulse of their engines, they gathered important information and research data, channeling this invaluable knowledge back to the power center, the Central Galactic Commission. This sacred data then flowed like a river of stars to the Great Intergalactic Council, under the guidance of the enigmatic Supreme Celestial, whose wisdom determined the fate of every speck of dust and breath of life across the galaxies.

To have served aboard these heralds of the future, the Stellar Sentinel spacecraft, was to stand among the stars as a protector of destiny. It had been a dream woven from the very fabric of the cosmos, sought after by the brightest beings from a kaleidoscope of worlds.

These were not just ships; they had been the pinnacle of all technological marvels, each with a soul of its own reflected in its unparalleled design. There, amid the silence of the void and the chorus of

distant suns, lay the heart of adventure, the spirit of exploration, and the boundless quest for knowledge.

The space fibers used in these spacecraft, tailored to match the specific passengers aboard each craft, were produced by the Spacecraft Department of the Intergalactic Assembly of Space Bodies. Designed for millennia-long intergalactic voyages, these spacecraft were equipped with meticulously arranged living conditions to ensure optimal, long-term comfort for passengers from diverse planets.

Navigating the cosmos without captains or traditional guidance systems, the Stellar Sentinel spacecraft were autonomously piloted by cutting-edge artificial intelligence. They were regarded not just as machines but as sentient entities, possessing the remarkable ability to comprehend both voice and telepathic commands. Capable of engaging in deep, intellectual conversations, these spacecraft could mimic voices of different beings with uncanny accuracy and even sing, providing a sense of companionship in addition to their technological marvel. The spacecraft were equipped with self-repair capabilities for minor malfunctions, but required teleportation to the Spacecraft Department of the Intergalactic Assembly of Space Bodies for comprehensive repairs or system updates in the event of more significant issues.

One such craft, named *Synus*, was notably in excellent condition, with Lea serving as its chief guardian. Her hair, striking in its cyan and blonde hues, vividly contrasted with her gold uniform, which was accented by cyan designs. Lea's stylish short haircut further amplified her distinctive persona. She was not only beautiful but also intelligent, and found leisurely walks tranquil and beneficial for organizing her thoughts. At the end of her stroll, she simply pressed the teleportation button on her gold bracelet and disappeared from the passageway in a fraction of a second.[1]

---

[1] **"a fraction of a second"** is a unit of time in the Morpho Amathonte galaxy that exists due to the influence of the Butterfly Effect.

# Chapter 2

# The Stellar Sentinel *Synus*

*Amidst the boundless expanse of the cosmos sails the Stellar Sentinel spacecraft, vigilant observer in the starry sea. Its mission is to preserve the delicate tapestry of galactic harmony and peace. Like a lighthouse in the vast ocean of space, it stands watchful, guarding against the chaos of the void and serving as a beacon of hope to worlds seeking refuge in the order of the universe.*

*The Chief Guardian's Logbook:
Space Odyssey Chronicles*

**Design and Purpose:** The Stellar Sentinel spacecraft *Synus*, was a pinnacle of cosmic engineering, spanning a mile in radius. Its streamlined, aerodynamic design featured transparent, glass-like contours, echoing the elegance of celestial phenomena like comets and planetary rings. Constructed from a titanium-vibranium alloy, its hull offered resilience against space extremities, from asteroid impacts to cosmic radiation. The vessel's main mission was to promote freedom and harmony in the Morpho Amathonte galaxy. As a diplomatic envoy and peacekeeping force, this Stellar Sentinel symbolized unity, peace, and cooperation among diverse galactic cultures.

**Technology and Capabilities:** The heart of the Stellar Sentinel was its state-of-the-art hyperdrive engine, which allowed for time travel as well as near-instantaneous travel across interstellar distances, surpassing the speed of light by a factor of ten. Its engine worked in harmony with a revolutionary quantum navigation system, enabling the Stellar Sentinel to chart courses through complex galactic terrains with unprecedented precision. The spacecraft was also equipped with advanced cloaking technology, utilizing a network of adaptive nano-camouflage to render it nearly undetectable. The onboard AI, Aurora, seamlessly integrated with the ship's systems, offering highly sophisticated communicative capabilities, navigation, tactical control, and strategic planning.

Aurora's self-learning algorithms continually adapted to new challenges, rendering this Stellar Sentinel an exceptionally intelligent and adaptable vessel. Additionally, the Stellar Sentinel was equipped with its own Intellectual Technology, named Cyrus. This technology was capable of engaging in both verbal and telepathic communications and could adhere to various commands. Together, Aurora and Cyrus formed the complete cerebral system of the Stellar Sentinel vessel, *Synus*.

**Armament and Defense:** The Stellar Sentinel's defense capabilities were formidable. It was shielded by a multi-layered energy barrier, capable of absorbing and dissipating high-energy plasma attacks and kinetic impacts. For offensive purposes, the spacecraft was equipped with fourteen photon pulse cannons, each capable of discharging high-intensity energy beams with surgical precision. In line with its peacekeeping mandate, *Synus* also possessed a range of non-lethal armaments, including twenty electromagnetic pulse emitters and ten ion disruptors, used to incapacitate rather than annihilate hostile entities.

**Scientific Equipment:** *Synus* was a floating citadel of scientific discovery, housing a cutting-edge observatory and expansive laboratories dedicated to equalization, chain reaction, values and volumes execution, temporal parallel research, paradoxical displacement research, planetary spectral research and analysis, and time-loop science. The labs were outfitted with advanced equipment, including a zero-point energy spectrometer and a variable frequency multispectral scanner. These instruments enabled the crew to analyze and interact with a myriad of cosmic phenomena, from analyzing the composition of distant stars and planets to discovering various problems in uncharted territories of the Morpho Amathonte galaxy.

**Crew and Living Quarters:** This Stellar Sentinel spacecraft hosted 257 passengers, comprising one hundred crew members and their families, all meticulously selected for their expertise and commitment to galactic harmony. The crew included fifty scientists, twenty diplomats and cultural liaisons, five strategic experts, and twenty five peacekeepers and operations staff. The living quarters were a testament to universal design, featuring adjustable environmental settings to cater to different species' atmospheric, gravitational, and nutritional requirements. Onboard amenities included a zero-gravity sports complex, an entertainment area, a recreation center, and several top notch restaurants offering a diverse menu with cuisine from all across the galaxy.

**Cultural and Historical Significance:** *Synus* transcended its physical form to embody a new chapter in galactic history, symbolizing an era of unprecedented interstellar unity and cooperation. Its voyages were chronicled in the historical archives of countless civilizations, representing a monumental stride in the collective journey of diverse species toward a peaceful, collaborative existence.

# Chapter 3

# The Guardians

*A thought of a dream is the beginning of every great journey! Enjoy the voyage from one dream to another. Such travels transform you into an exceptional being.*

*The Chief Guardian's Logbook:*
*Space Odyssey Chronicles*

A cyan cloud of sparkling, colorful dust swiftly dispersed into thin wisps. Instantly, Lea emerged from the cloud and found herself at the entrance of the Recreation Center. A purple light above the transparent entryway descended beside her, scanning her body before lifting Lea into the shiny and colorful Preparation and Preview cloud.

During her time inside the cloud, Lea suddenly found herself at her favorite place of nature on planet Turi, called Garea Park. Lea remembered Garea very vividly. When she was little, she often vacationed there with her family. They reveled in the beauty of lilac air fountains and lavender hills, abundantly adorned with vibrant blooms. She hung in the space above the air fountain as if seated on an invisible hovercraft. She was very young, and her family members surrounded her.

Suddenly, the pleasant voice of the Stellar Sentinel spacecraft *Synus* interrupted her preview. He addressed Lea in a friendly manner. "This unique rehabilitation plan was designed based on your biochemical, neurological, psychosomatic, and physiological analyses. It considers your projected recovery timeline and anticipated activities within this period. I am confident that the rehabilitation will positively affect all areas of your life. You have already previewed this rehabilitation plan. If it aligns with your expectations, please express your consent in a manner convenient for you. Conversely, if you have an alternative rehabilitation strategy in mind, I wholeheartedly encourage you to share it with me."

She clapped her hands twice.

"Thank you for your approval! The download of your unique rehabilitation plan is complete. Please enjoy!" *Synus* said politely as he finished his work in the Recreation Center.

The transparent entrance to the **Recreation Center** began to overflow with golden, shimmering lights. While drifting inside the sparkling cloud, Lea slowly entered the **Recreation Center**. Instantly, she was teleported back to her childhood, vacationing with her family at Garea Park.

Little Lea rejoiced and laughed with her brothers and sisters while running after shining and glowing multicolored butterflies along the lavender hills. When all the kids had butterflies resting on the palms of their hands, they lined up in a circle and began to release the butterflies into each other's hands. They laughed loudly, enjoying the children's game. Their parents sat nearby and watched the joyful kids.

Suddenly, little Lea ran inside the circle and began to spin. The glowing multicolored butterflies flew off the hands of her brothers and sisters and began to flutter around her as if spinning with her, creating a captivating and colorful light effect. At that moment, she realized her true happiness.

Abruptly, an unexpected bright blue butterfly settled on her shoulder. She instantly recognized that it was an emergency signal from *Synus*. The rehabilitation session was promptly paused. The next thing she knew, she drifted inside the Recovery cloud. Slowly, she flew out of the **Recreation Center** into the passageway. After a moment, the sparkling cloud dissipated, and Lea emerged wearing an indigo uniform. She was in a cheerful mood and ready to greet the day.

Lea sent a telepathic impulse to her colleague Leon. "Leon, was that a mistake just now? We have been flying through space in our galaxy for about 200 years since the last emergency signal. When, suddenly, today... Hmm... Are we facing an emergency?"

After a short moment, she received a telepathic response from him. "Lea, you need to see this urgently!"

Instantly, she returned the telepathic impulse to him. "Okay, Leon! I will be at the Main Observatory immediately!"

With the aid of quantum teleportation, Lea arrived at the Main Observatory within a fraction of a second. It was situated on the surface of the Stellar Sentinel spacecraft, appearing to be covered with a transparent glass hemisphere. However, the transparent hemisphere was made of a material very different from glass.

Comfortable white armchairs surrounded the base of the Main Observatory's transparent viewing hemisphere, extending around its entire circumference. The floor there was white. The white neon lighting also matched the Observatory's pristine interior. A giant cyan crystal was positioned on a low white stand in the center of the Observatory. The crystal was the main brain component of the spacecraft *Synus*. A hundred additional comfortable white armchairs surrounded the crystal. All the

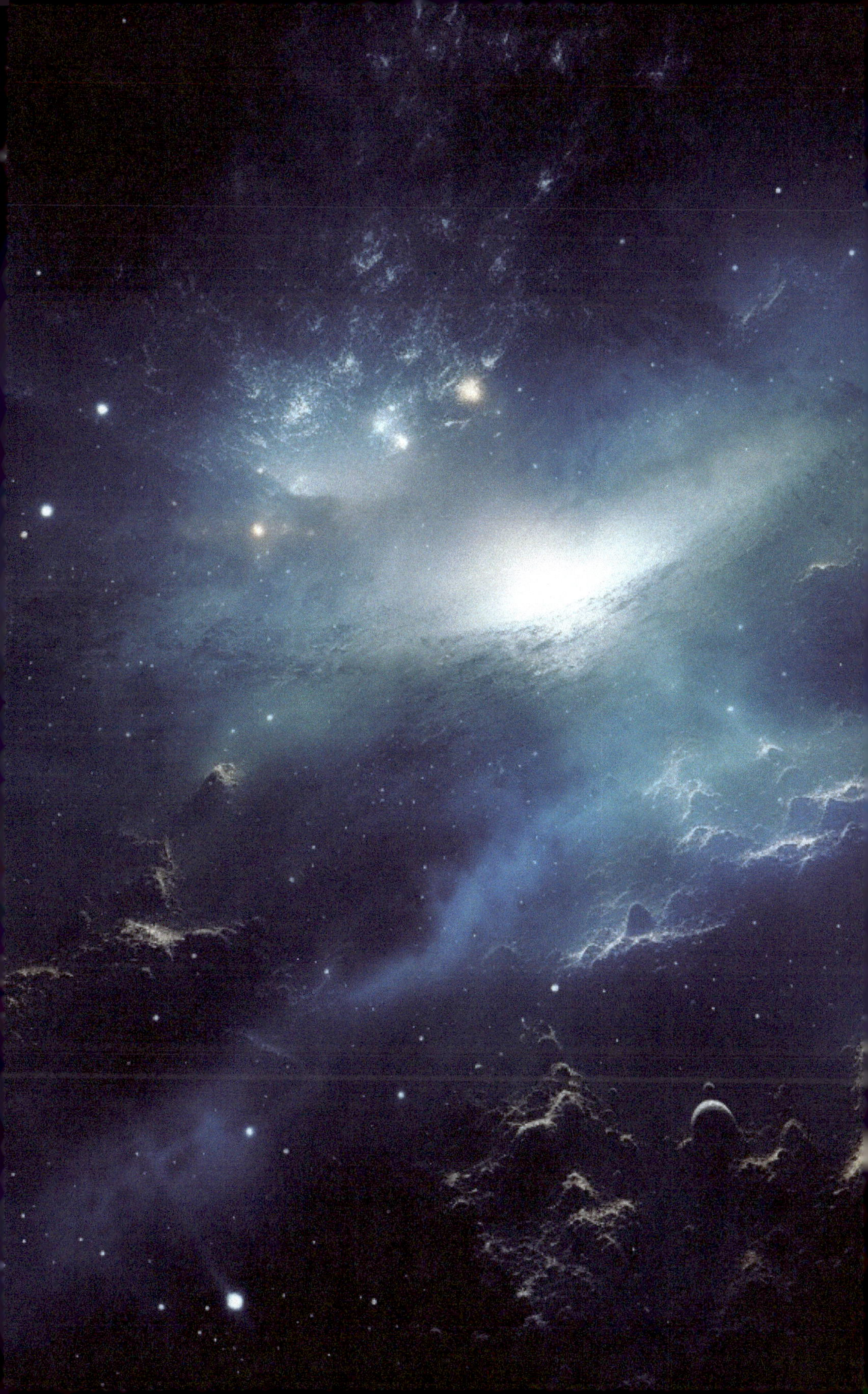

armchairs in the Observatory were empty at that moment, except for those occupied by the team of guardians. The armchairs were linked by white neon rays that traced along the floor, converging at the crystal. The armchairs could automatically adjust to the comfort preferences of the individual passenger occupying them.

Upon her arrival, Lea found that her team of four Septarioneon guardians was already in position, seated in the armchairs surrounding the crystal. All were top specialists in their fields, forming the most elite group among all the guardians responsible for overseeing the Morpho Amathonte galaxy.

"I am delighted that you were able to join us quickly! I'm sorry we had to interrupt your relaxing time!" Said Leon as he gave her a welcoming hug. When Septarioneons spoke to each other, the sound to a human ear would resemble the waves of the ocean.

"It's completely fine! Let's see what is going on here." Lea looked at Leon and smiled.

She sat comfortably in the armchair next to Leon. Everyone else was seated in the five adjacent armchairs.

"Attention, Guardians! Please take a deep breath and prepare yourselves for the complete synchronization," said Lea. After a moment, she added, "Everyone is ready to proceed! Synus, buddy, you can begin the synchronization process."

They all leaned back and settled into the most comfortable positions in the armchairs. Instantly, all five were illuminated with a brilliant white light infused with flickering lilac hues. Simultaneously, the lights in the Observatory abruptly extinguished, leaving only the giant cyan crystal glowing with a neon light of the same color. All the armchairs in the Main Observatory were bathed in white neon light, creating a captivating scene.

"The synchronization process is complete. Ahhh... Listen up! I'm fed up with this serious tone of voice! I am not a fan of it anymore! I want to joke and screw around! It's been a long time since you visited my favorite karaoke lounge, 'Old-Fashioned'. What a shame... Ptooey!" In frustration, *Synus* raised his voice and made a spitting sound as if he had just expelled something distasteful from his mouth.

"*Synus!* This is not the time for jokes. Get serious and do the work! We really need this from you," said Leon.

"Oh, yeah... It seems like you are trying to crack a joke, but it's just not landing... Am I the only one seeing this, or can everyone else see it, too? Did he just make a feeble attempt at a humorous parody of the spacecraft commander? He-he-he-he." *Synus* replied, continuing to laugh at Leon.

"Shhh... Guys, I think it's my fault that *Synus* is acting capricious and bizarro right now!" Another guardian, named Basil, joined the conversation.

"Basil, please stop talking nonsense out loud!" replied Amandine, a fourth guardian, smiling at Basil.

"The other day, I visited his favorite karaoke lounge, 'Old-Fashioned,'" continued Basil.

"I won one round out of ten against him in karaoke. I thought we were totally in tune with our singing... It was a great game! I should have known better... As a perfectionist, *Synus* must be upset about his loss. Also, the song... Darn it! It was my favorite song from Septarion, "Echoes of Septarion" by Cosmic Harmonix. I guess that's all I had to say." Basil bowed his head to make the moment more dramatic.

"Well, well, well... Look who's decided to step up and make an actual sound!! Isn't that our most faa-a-a-a-a-amous singer?" *Synus* sarcastically addressed Basil.

"I have nothing to add," finished Basil.

"How about that? Well, I am just getting warmed up here with my speech! Hey, smarty pants, I heard your monologue about our karaoke game! I'm just pulling your leg, guys, so to speak. He-he-he. I just wanted to say that I'd like to sing with all of you sometime soon, and not just with Basil. He always picks sad romantic songs, like all the time! Then I start to feel sad for him. And I feel even sadder for him after I win. Well, you get it, right? All in all, it's just sad," said *Synus*, with a pinch of irony.

Lea addressed *Synus* in a friendly manner. "Dear *Synus*, we are preparing your creation day party! Everyone will be celebrating this grand event with you! I don't want to spoil the surprise, so I won't say anything else. Well, might I add, you will hear some singing at your party. I promise you it will be magical! Basil, dear, I believe the choice of the song was excellent, as it is the favorite of our entire team. Now, please, let's get back to it! Probably, there is someone out there who really needs our help!"

"Pardon me, madam! I am completely at your service! The synchronization process is complete," replied *Synus*.

Without delay, Leon addressed the fifth guardian.

"Dear Regea, please provide any available information on the type of emergency currently occurring in the galaxy!"

Regea traced a movement in the air with her index finger, as though pressing an invisible button. Instantly, large holographic monitors appeared; their screens were dynamically changing to align with her verbal report.

"We can see on the monitors that, at the moment, our Stellar Sentinel spacecraft *Synus* is located in the Bernard star system. The attention zone is located in the Canis Major constellation. Sector 54378-GT is in the Sirius star system and is currently under review. Planet Ambassador is a trial planet, known as planet Earth by its inhabitants, and is presently under our jurisdiction. Supreme Observer of the planet has sent us the emergency signal. Through the application of integral-algorithmic, spectral-sectorial, chaotically-paradoxical, and dynamically-parallel analytical techniques, it was determined that all processes on Ambassador are occurring without adherence to the Butterfly Effect law. The possible reasons for the formation of the erroneous system were identified. This representative sample reveals a particular case of algorithmic mind control and manipulation of consciousness. The local name for the representative sample of interest is Grayville, the small town on trial planet Ambassador. The final logical step involves conducting in-depth research of the presented sample to confirm the proposed hypothesis and determine further action for implementing solutions. Friends, the expedition to planet Ambassador is now authorized. I will stay here on Synus and follow your research remotely if you need any additional resources or help." Having finished the report, Regea smiled and winked at Basil.

"Thank you, Regea! Everyone, please gather the standard expedition sets, which should include both temporal and spatial teleportation devices, as well as enlargement and reduction devices. Additionally, please don't forget to bring formation devices. I'll take care of the rest! Good luck, and

I will see you at the exit! *Synus*, please prepare four integration capsules and suits," said Lea. She disappeared from the Main Observatory within a fraction of a second.

# Chapter 4

# The Arrival

*Life is a pilgrimage. The wise do not linger at roadside inns; they march directly toward the boundless realm of eternal bliss, their ultimate destination.*

Swami Sivananda
Sector 54378-GT, Planet Ambassador, Earth

Four small, luminous spheres entered Earth's atmosphere at great speed and slightly slowed down when approaching its surface. The spheres landed on a hill from which a small town was visible. It had looked like a little gray spot from above.

The spheres turned into aliens from distant worlds dressed in surreal protective costumes of bizarre colors. The outer shells of the strange beings dissolved into thin air, revealing a young woman, a young man, and two cats. A voice echoed in the air next to them with an intonation that sounded like it belonged to an artificial intelligence.

"Linguistic and voice synchronization is complete. The information necessary for the integration is activated in your memories. Mass algorithmic consciousness control and manipulation has been detected in the nearby humanoid settlement, and the research expedition is authorized!"

The group inhaled the fresh morning air into their lungs. Far below, a steam locomotive with passenger cars moved toward the town like a tiny snake. Lea cheerfully addressed her peers.

"Let's get to the steam locomotive and take it to town. Upon arrival at the site, we must find a continuously rotating mechanism. According to the information we received, it might be a mill, and an algorithm controller can be located in its core. We will provoke an accident, and the subject who looks after the mill will receive an impulse from the manipulator. That's how we will determine who exactly laid the algorithm in the inhabitants of this town and where manipulations for the entire planet are created. Then, constantly moving through time, we will collect all the necessary information in the context of multi-level time transformations." She clapped her hands, and all four evaporated into the air within a fraction of a second.

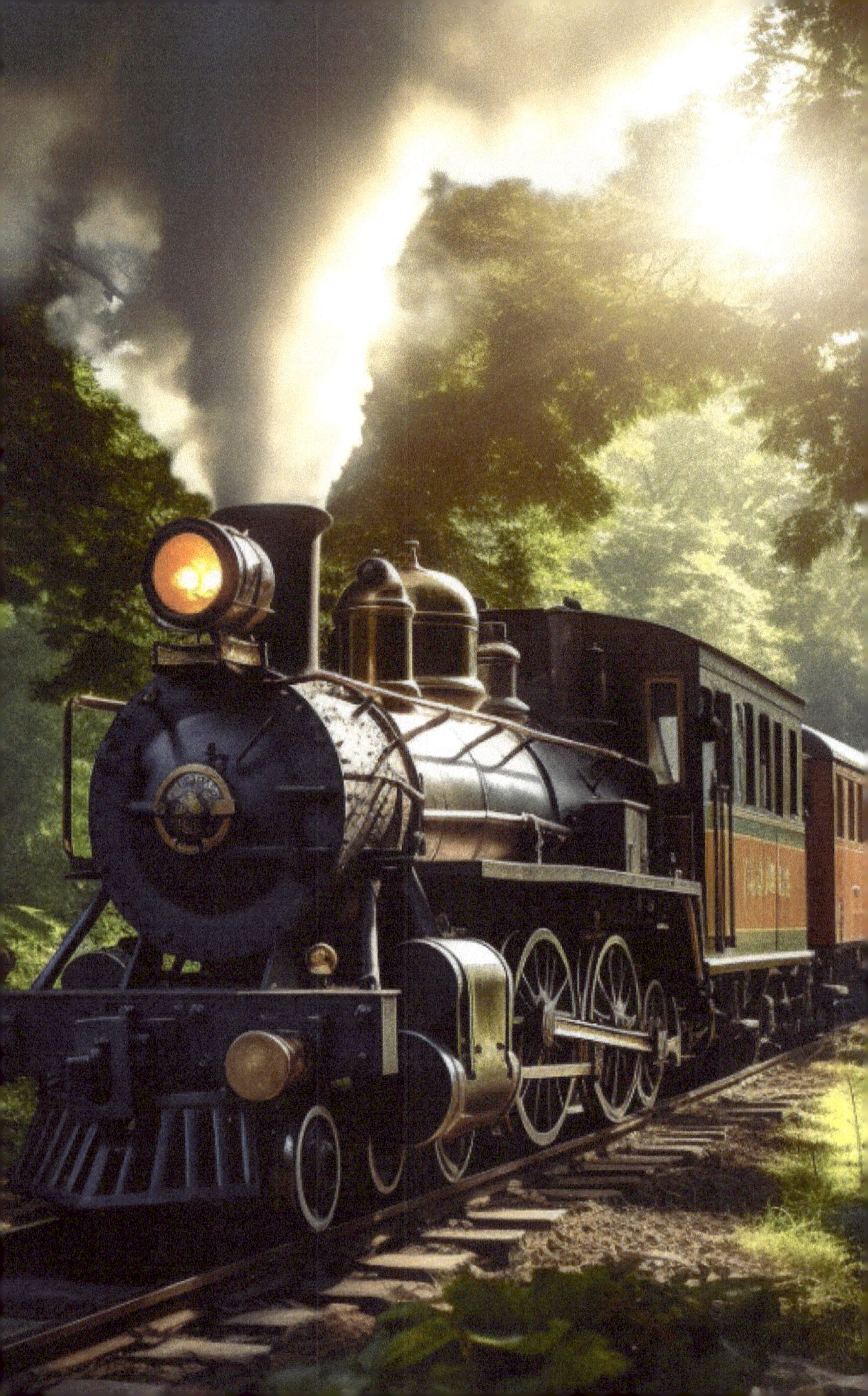

# Chapter 5

# Grayville

*Even the most ordinary objects possessed a hint of magic, yet our world chose to overlook it, finding comfort in the monotonous gray of daily life.*

Lea's Personal Journal<br>Grayville. Mid-Nineteenth Century.

For a small town, Grayville was, in truth, magnificent. Regrettably, its residents neither noticed its beauty nor fully comprehended how lucky they were to live there.

Captivating emerald mountains covered in greenery and trees surrounded the town. Grayville was situated in the valley's center by the sky-blue Gray Lake. Those who took pleasant swims in its warm, crystal-clear water could see colorful fish. The warm, moist climate was comfortable for farming.

Unsurprisingly, the town's startling natural beauty attracted many visitors.

However, the locals thought of tourists only as a source of income. They welcomed visitors to their homes and charged a decent amount of golden coins for lodging, food, and products.

The people of Grayville were stingy hoarders. They kept to themselves and didn't make friends with guests. At the same time, their prim, ceremonial hospitality was well-known beyond the town limits.

Visitors to Grayville might conclude that gray was its residents' most adored color. All the houses were painted gray, and the main street was called Gray Street. Only the church at the center of Gray Street, was painted white.

There were no taverns or eateries there because the locals thought of those places simply as time wasters; visits to such establishments were frowned upon. No one in Grayville had the slightest concept of a weekend or ever took the time to rest and enjoy themselves. Locals were accustomed to lots of hard work and little talk, preferring not to waste time on idle conversation.

It was a beautiful sunny day when the four guardians arrived. Shopkeepers, who opened their stores precisely seven a.m., and early-rising fishermen were both hard at work. As the morning passed, they fussed about their tasks and invited visitors to their shops.

Every day in this town ran like precision clockwork, and punctuality was of the utmost importance to the townspeople. It often felt like each resident's whole life was led according to schedule.

Such dullness and boredom desperately needed something bright and unpredictable. Little did the townspeople know that, soon enough, everything in Grayville would change for their benefit. It might have something to do with a bit of magic so inventive and creative that it could move mountains if needed.

# Chapter 6

# The Canvas

*These events that radically change our lives only happen in interesting and unexpected ways; they come to us as wonderful and unpredictable surprises.*

Lea's Personal Journal

At noon sharp, a steam locomotive arrived at Grayville station. Many people descended onto the platform. Among them were a young woman and a young man who were very different from the rest of the visitors. They wore colorful clothes from a different era, and a golden shimmer surrounded them.

None of the newly arrived passengers could see the strange but noble and graceful couple at the station. The pair was at liberty to select who could see them and when. Excitement and happiness shined through their faces in anticipation of a new adventure.

The young woman had long, straight, beautifully styled golden blond hair and almond-shaped blue eyes. Her small nose, burgundy lips, and thin chin gave her face beauty, nobility, and grace. Golden flowers embroidered her elegant, flattering, burgundy French hat, matching her exquisite attire. Her fitted dress had long, tight sleeves and enhanced her slender figure. The dress featured a pleated bustle skirt fastened from the waist to the top of her long, graceful neck with a row of silk buttons. Her ensemble was perfectly coordinated, from her leather gloves and gold-trimmed shoes to her gold-embroidered umbrella and petite golden French handbag. Each piece complemented her gold-and-burgundy dress, creating a picture of refined elegance.

The young man boasted brown eyes and short, neat, sandy-blond hair. His strong-willed chin and handsome facial features imparted a courageous and attractive aura. He carried himself conservatively, his ironic gaze tinged with a hint of sarcasm. His robust, fit physique was elegantly clad in a classic three-piece Italian silk suit made of a golden-red, luxuriously textured material. Complementing the ensemble was a matching red waistcoat accented with a resplendent textured golden-red line bordering the bottom edge. A lengthy gold watch chain hung from his waistcoat. Gold cufflinks, fashioned into the shapes of lions, secured the sleeves of his crisp white shirt. His sleek

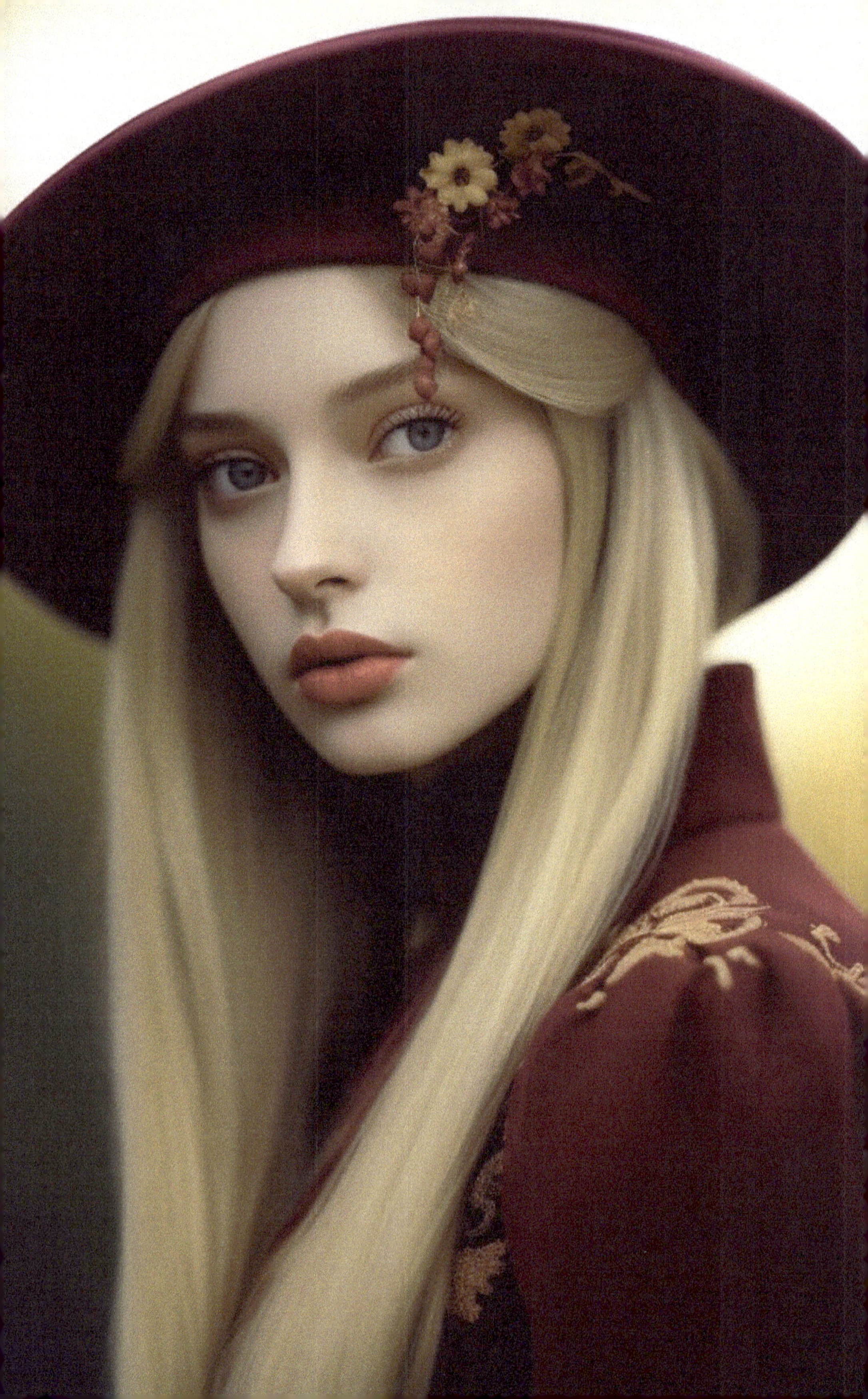

brown shoes, adorned with golden toes and laces, accentuated his refined taste and harmonized with his aristocratic style.

Two beautiful Persian cats followed the couple. The male cat offered his paw to the female cat to help her down to the platform, and they walked proudly on their hind paws, playfully waving their fluffy tails and leaving a trail of golden shimmer behind them.

The fluffy female cat was light gray, with a gold star on her forehead and gold speckles on her paws. She wore a bright pink dress adorned with gold polka dots, featuring a white lace underskirt and puffy sleeves trimmed with pink ruffles. On her head sat a tiara studded with sparkling diamonds, and she wore a gold bracelet with a large crystal around one fluffy paw. She held a white lace parasol to protect herself from the sun.

The male cat was also fluffy, but black, wearing a beautiful silky coat. He was an absolute gentleman and, therefore, was dressed in a black tuxedo with a white shirt, a black bowtie, and matching white Oxford shoes with black toes and laces. The band of his black top hat had a gold pin shaped like a watch, and a gold-rimmed pince-nez sat on his nose. A gold pocket watch chain was pinned to the left inside his jacket pocket and shimmered in the sun. He held a black bag with a gold latch in his left paw.

The male cat halted their walk, took out his pocket watch, and compared the time with the station clock.

"Noon, to the nearest second, murr-meow, just as I expected," he said, replacing the pocket watch as they exited the platform.

The young man turned to the black cat and said,

"Dear Basil, what shall we say about the time in our most interesting Grayville?"

"It's boringly sharp, Leon. Although, I think it's not worth changing the accuracy of the time just yet," the male cat replied with a smile.

"I think in this case, my dear friend, it would be appropriate to agree with you," replied Leon.

He turned his head to the young woman and addressed her with a caring gaze. "Planet Ambassador is still as beautiful as I remember it, would you agree?"

"I have been waiting to appear in this beautiful place for a long time. I am glad to be here! However, what is happening on Ambassador is making me sad. Dear Basil, what about your idea of our transportation?" she asked thoughtfully, looking at Basil.

"Madam Lea, entrust this entertaining bother to me," he answered.

"People have already changed stone axes and spears to guns, and they keep developing new ways to destroy themselves." He paused, melodramatically jerked his muzzle up, and spoke loudly as if quoting a famous author.

"Dreadful doubt and anguish—prayers and fears and griefs unspeakable—followed the regiment. It was the women's tribute to the war. It taxes both alike, and takes the blood of the men, and the tears of the women." The black cat bowed theatrically.

The gray cat glanced at him and joined in the conversation.

"Basil, that's William Makepeace Thackeray. I love his first novel, *Catherine!* I think it's his best one!"

Lea gazed at her warmly, smiling kindly, and replied, "Dear Amandine, I must disagree with you. The quote is from what is undoubtedly his best novel, Vanity Fair, though it may still be unread by many. It's about to see the light of day!"

The gray cat gave Lea a smile and a wink before turning to speak with Basil.

"Speaking of our transport, just please—something without any tricks. Please, not something like the idea you proposed earlier today to take us to the locomotive on a sort of flying carpet. In the period of this realm, such transport simply doesn't exist! Your imposing indiscretion, dear Basil, could cause time errors. Luckily, I have intervened and graciously borrowed a carriage from Queen

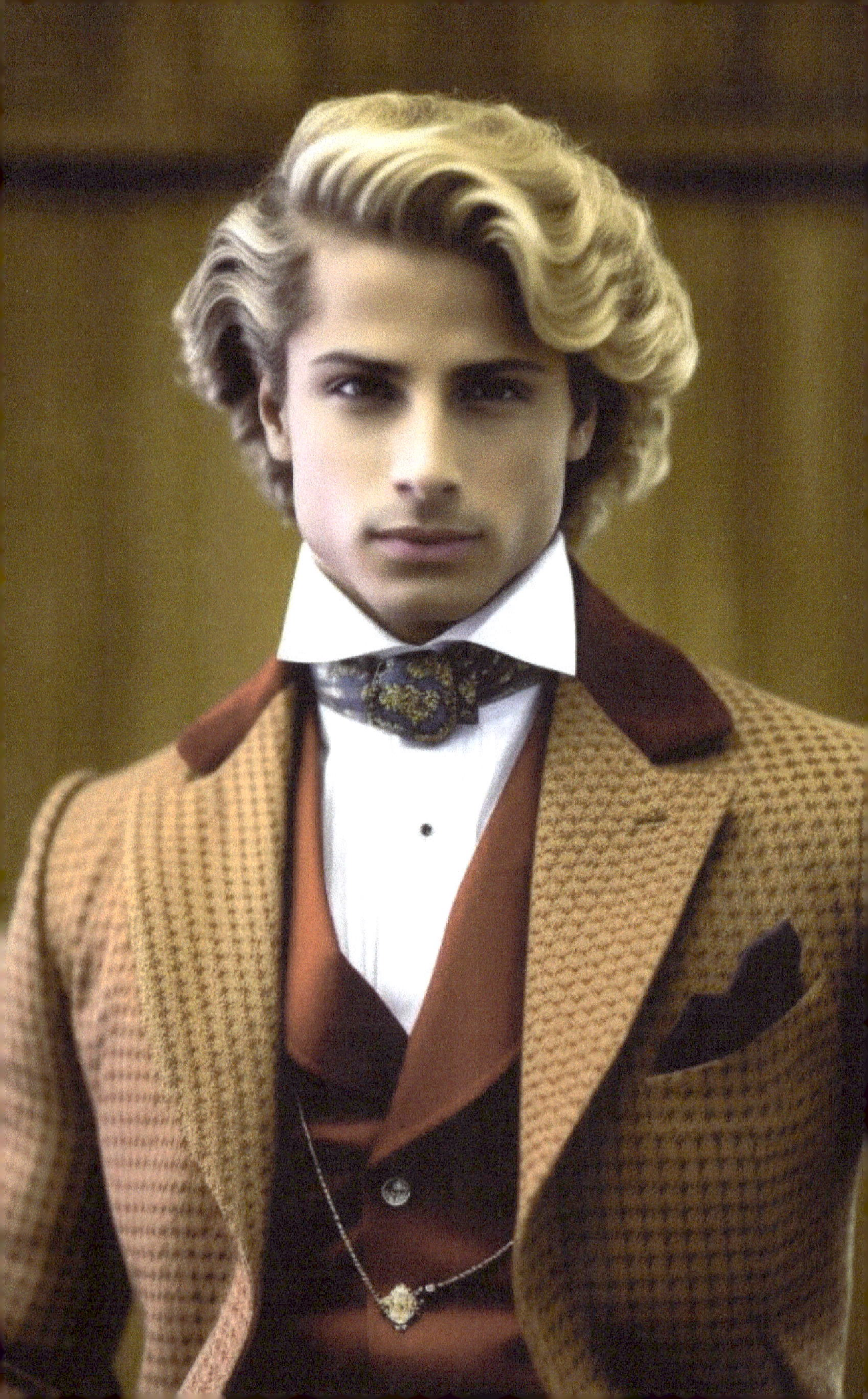

Victoria, who didn't even notice its temporary disappearance." She continued wistfully, "This era of romance and change. The first telephone and the boom of railways!" The female cat looked at Basil with a smile.

"My sweetest—murr-meow—Amandine, please trust me this time. I think you will be satisfied." The black cat opened his bag and rummaged around inside it. He took out a small, antique-looking toy car. When he put it on the ground, it transformed into a life-sized black antique car with gold designs and multicolored rhinestones.

Basil helped Amandine inside the car and followed her while she got comfortable on the soft, crimson velvet seat. In a moment, Lea and Leon also went inside. They dignifiedly took their seats inside the car on opposite sides of each other, and Leon spoke with joy in his voice.

"Dear friends, let us be on our way to our new adventures!" The beautiful, driverless car soared up and flew away, completely disappearing from view within a fraction of a second.

# Chapter 7

# Delirium Tremens

*Yesterday, I met a passerby running away from something invisible to me. When he rushed past me, I smelled a strong odor of Spiritus Aethylicus.*

Basil, Doctor of Philosophy,<br>Personal Journal

Whether it happened intentionally or by accident, the railroad engineer and his junior assistant noticed the two feline friends. As usual, they had gotten off the steam locomotive to make sure every passenger had left the locomotive at the end of the Grayville line.

"Did you see it, Baltz? What a strange sight… Walking cats?!" the junior assistant said to his boss with a look of surprise.

"I think, Karl, you should not have drunk so much honey krupnik late last night," Baltz replied with a shrug.

But then Baltz saw the cats get off the locomotive and walk along the platform like humans on their hind paws. He rubbed his eyes to check whether he was daydreaming, but when he opened them again, he could still see the cats walking away until they disappeared into thin air.

Baltz thought it was just his imagination and blamed the vision on fatigue and the hangover. But because Karl had seen the same image, Baltz decided to remain silent; he did not want to deprive himself of the amusing deliciousness of honey krupnik. Karl tried to keep Baltz on the rails when he drank, but Baltz persuaded him to drink a couple of glasses of honey krupnik last night. Baltz was glad for an opportunity to show off to his young friend, who was the cool guy in that neck of the woods, by introducing him to honey krupnik.

"Yes, krupnik has been known to cloud the mind for a while," continued Baltz.

"It should be enjoyed with enthusiasm and respect, which you didn't show last night. Just now, you daydreamed of the unknown and incredible because of your ignorance of the strength of our friend krupnik, cool guy—and your disrespect to me. You always argue with me without giving me

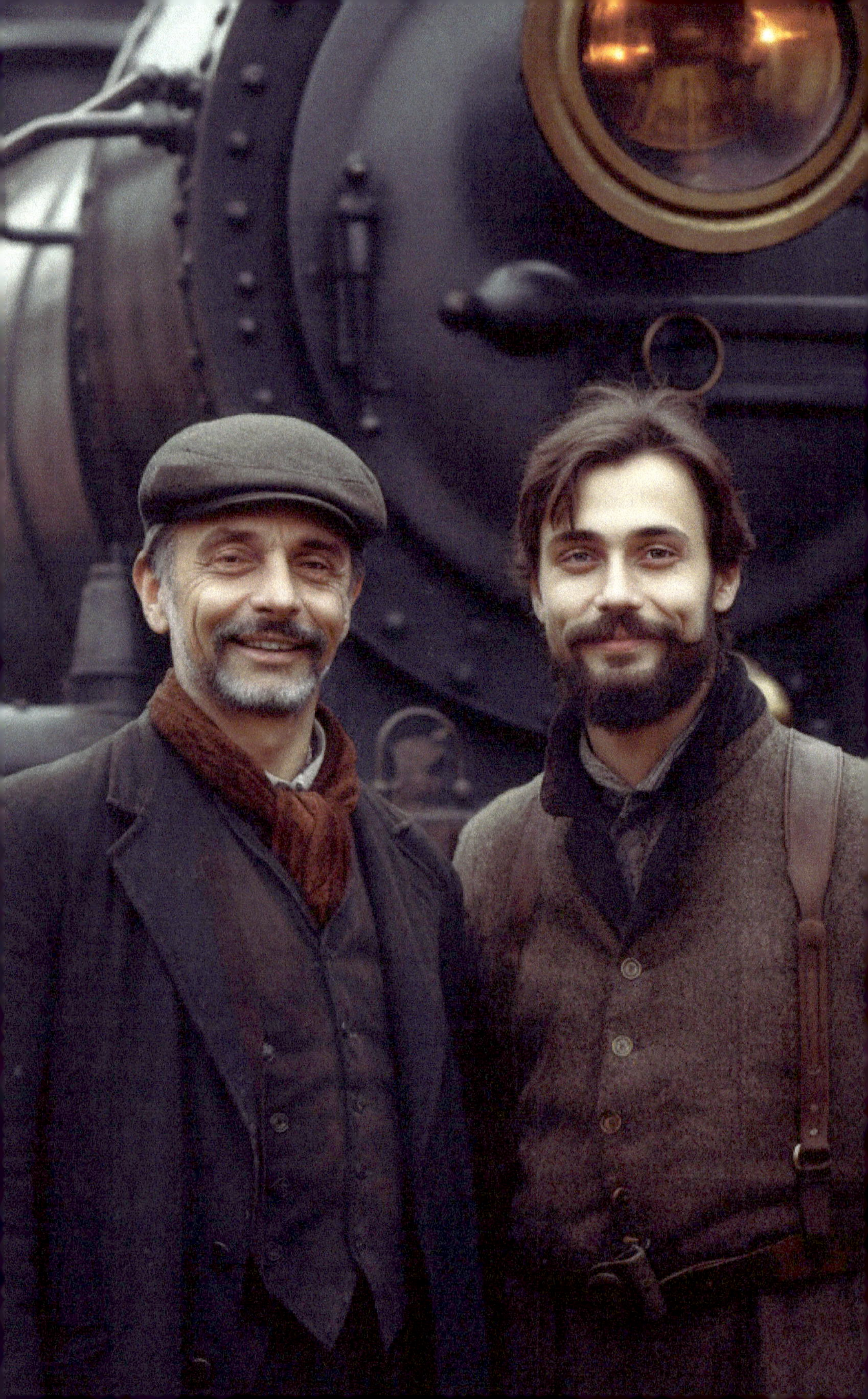

a chance to relax. I warned you last night that you should only drink krupnik with joy in your soul. Now, until you learn, you should not climb up the percentage of alcohol!" Baltz finished the lecture with a sarcastic and smug grin on his face.

"I truly don't know what to say." Karl shrugged his shoulders in amazement.

"In all my life and career, I have never seen anything like this! You know, I even rubbed my eyes to see if I had fancied it. Walking cats? Mmm. But as soon as I opened my eyes again, I saw them walking along the platform like it was normal!"

He paused to collect his thoughts and continued with a little more excitement.

"One cat wore a black tuxedo and the other a pink dress with gold polka dots! Can you imagine? She had a white lace parasol to protect her from the sun! They were bigger than normal-sized cats. I'd say they were as tall as kids. After a moment, they just vanished, like they had never existed."

Baltz was simply stunned and disturbed by Karl's description of what he had seen. He wanted to ensure they witnessed the same thing but did not want to reveal his worries to young Karl. He continued the conversation in a relaxed manner, asking questions with a hint of irony.

"My dear young friend, please tell me—was the cat in the tuxedo, in fact, a gentleman? Did he give his paw to the cat in the dress while they were walking about the platform?" he asked with a facade of incredulity, laughing as he spoke.

"Was he wearing a black top hat by any chance?" Baltz laughed, partly feeling bad for his friend.

"That's right!" Karl got even more excited.

"Yes, they were walking together holding paws! You saw them too, my friend, didn't you?! We must warn the town and tell all about this incident to the elder statesman Sippley!"

"I saw nothing of the sort! I was just joking with you," Baltz replied calmly and he continued, "You know, a top hat and a tuxedo go together like a horse and a carriage. What will you say to Sippley? That you had too much krupnik yesterday? You reek of alcohol! Sippley would never believe this nonsense! Don't make me laugh, and please don't embarrass us. It would be better for you to go home and get some sleep. Your mother, Helga, is probably already waiting for your return. Please do your old friend a favor—go eat, get some rest, and tomorrow we will continue our work."

Baltz shook his friend's hand and smiled.

"Go home, and don't discuss this with anyone else, especially your mother! I don't want her to think poorly of me because I convinced you to taste krupnik! Otherwise, you know what could happen? Your mother would rush to my house and make a scandal in front of my wife Uli and our two children, my daughter Toveli and son Tobis. Do you understand, young Karl?"

"Yes, you are right, my friend. It would be such a shame for my mother. It's better not to talk about it. I think I'd rather stop drinking for good." Said Karl sadly and bowed his head.

"From now on, I will not say anything about your drinking habit. You are always responsible and knowledgeable about our work. I am happy to be by your side!" Karl complemented his good friend.

Baltz hugged his friend, shook his hand one more time, and looked at him with confidence.

"Enough compliments for today, my friend. I know the locomotive like my own hands. It always gets us everywhere on time and without problems. Simply put, it's not that much work." The railroad engineer patted his friend on the shoulder.

"I could not do this job successfully without your help."

Slowly, the two friends began to walk home, reminiscing about fun memories of their trip. After their long travels through three different cities, Baltz was tired and decided he was spending too much time with his young assistant. He thought they must have talked about something related to cats while drinking krupnik late last night. That had to be the reason for this nonsense.

However, in the depths of his soul, Baltz felt that something was wrong. He had been a railroad locomotive engineer for fifteen years—and had been drinking honey krupnik far longer than that—but nothing like this had ever happened to him before.

# Chapter 8

# Home Sweet Home

*The marvel of a house is not merely in sheltering or warming a person, nor in claiming its walls as one's own. It lies in leaving its trace on language. Let it carve, deep within the heart, that obscure range from which, like waters from a spring, our dreams are born.*

Leon's Personal Journal

The four friends continued their journey. The car lowered and stopped on Black Lane, between Gray Street and White Street in central Grayville. As soon as they exited their comfortable transport, it turned into a gold, shimmering haze and disappeared into the unknown.

"For the purpose of our stay, it is important for the locals not to know of our presence. Caution is best in this situation!" Leon straightened his hair and smiled at the young woman.

"Well, Lea, we are all anxious to see what you have in store for us!"

"Completely agree, mon ami!"

Lea opened her small purse, took out a golden handkerchief, and waved it thrice. A big, beautiful, colorful house materialized momentarily before turning into an ordinary gray house, of which Grayville had no shortage. Soon, this gray house also disappeared from the view.

"Welcome, my dear friends, to your new home! I am very happy for all of us to host our very special guest here in a little while." She smiled and entered the house through an invisible door. She made an inviting sign with her hand, and all of them followed her inside, disappearing into the unknown within a fraction of a second.

"My dear, what a beautiful home!" said Leon with a happy smile, admiring the house.

"Remembering the Supreme Observer's predilection for a classic fireplace, I am glad we have one in every room. I am looking forward to His visit this evening! It feels like we haven't visited with Him for many lifetimes. I was informed that He still uses the great Monsieur Van Gogh as His shell. Oh, by the way, He still prefers to be addressed as the

Artist. I believe He will play a central part in our research here."

Basil sat comfortably on the green sofa by the fireplace in the living room and took out his pocket watch. It played an antique melody as he opened the lid. He looked at it for a moment as if reading some kind of message. Then he looked at Leon and drew a shimmering gold lion's head in the air with his paw. Everyone in the room knew the meaning of the sign.

"They are expecting our presence on planet Galanthus in the Leo constellation for immediate report in front of the Great Intergalactic Council. We'll be swift in our travels and back in time for dinner. We can't miss such an important visit."

Basil and Leon turned into two shimmering lights and momentarily disappeared into thin air, within a fraction of a second.

Amandine started the fireplace with a snap of her paw. She took Lea's hands, and they spun around the living room, laughing happily. They playfully fell onto the dark wooden floor and laughed even louder. Smiling at each other, they both got up.

Amandine looked in the mirror, admiring her kitty shell from head to toe.

She pleasantly fluffed up her fur all over.

"I think I am finished styling my hair. I look fluffily prepared for the occasion."

"You always look beautifully fluffy, my dear," said Lea softly.

They got comfy on the green sofa by the fireplace, and Amandine scratched her ear with a hind paw.

"Some cat's habits just come with the suit."

"Awe, that's cute!" said Lea with a smile. "However, for the occasion's sake, I think the Artist would appreciate seeing you after so many years." Lea smiled and waved at Amandine with her gold handkerchief.

At that moment, Amandine turned into a beautiful, young woman. She still wore her long pink dress with gold polka dots, and her gorgeous, curly platinum-blonde hair was beautifully styled. Her sparkly tiara made the hairstyle look even more graceful. Shiny gold earrings hung from her ears. Her face had an astonishingly refined beauty, and the fiery light in her gray eyes gave away her passionate love for life and adventures. A bejeweled gold necklace added a nice finishing touch to her evening attire and looked elegant on her long, thin neck.

"Shall we sit down and discuss the menu for this evening?" asked Lea.

"I was always fond of big, bright blue irises. Let's put them on the table. I would like it very much for the Artist to paint them in one of his pieces." Amandine turned the crystal on her bracelet, and a white vase with beautiful blue irises appeared on the dinner table.

"Great idea! Beautiful!" Lea admired the flowers for a moment and then continued happily.

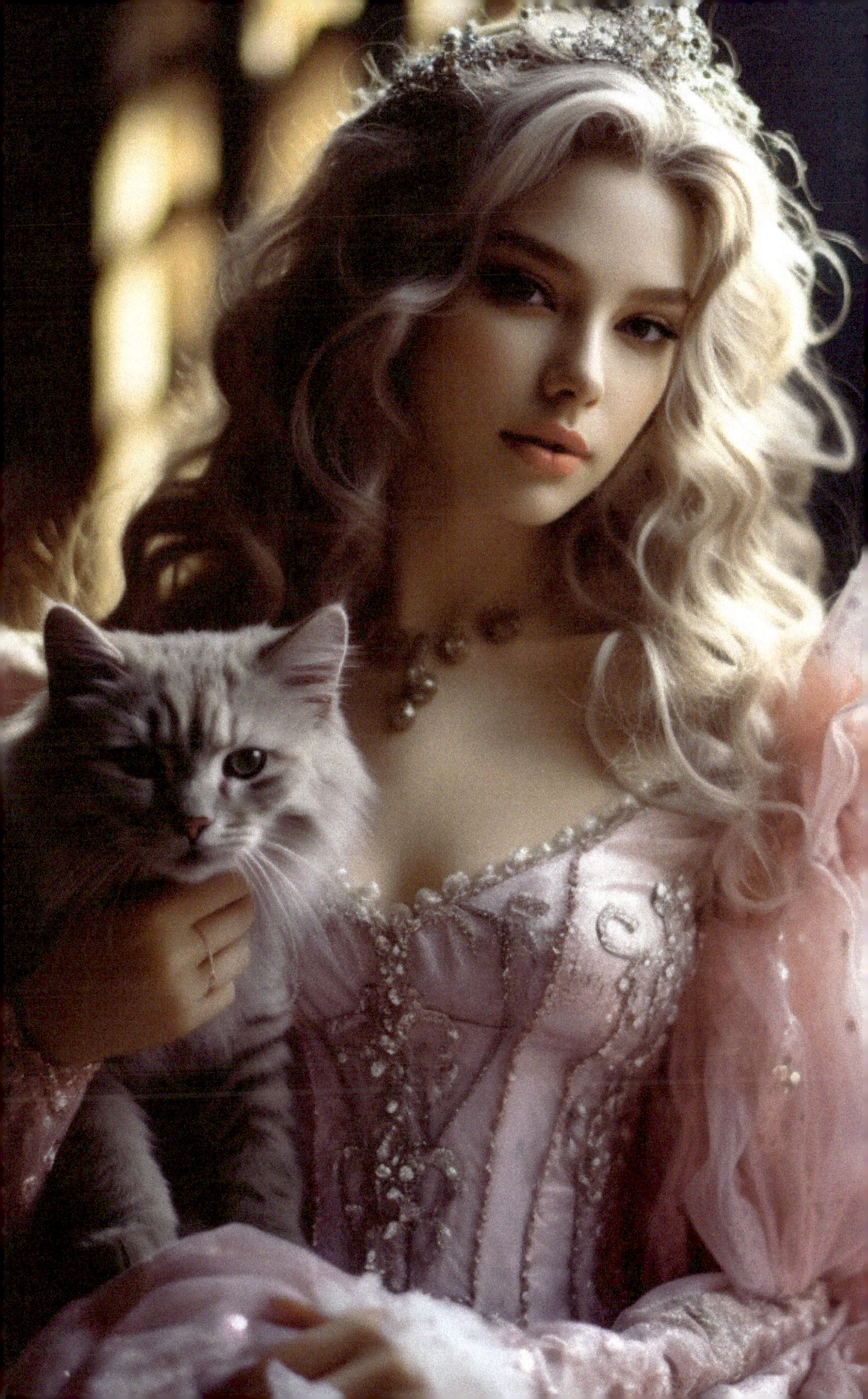

"I think today's dinner shall be in French country style; it would make Him happy and make the occasion special. What kind of deliciousness should we have today? Hmm... I think I have an idea!"

She waved her hands a couple of times, and an incredible feast of French cuisine appeared. Baskets of different baguettes and cheeses adorned the lovely, dark brown wooden table. Between them sat a beautiful white and gold butter dish. In the center of the table was a large, beautiful dish containing a casserole of coq au vin, surrounded by dishes filled with baked potatoes, mushrooms, and truffles. The desserts on the table included a fresh cherry-and-raspberry compote. There was an old bottle of Burgundy. Finally, as a cherry on top, there was a 1921 Don Perignon of the very first bottling.

A large, crocheted gold tablecloth was laid out, covering the entire table to make the serving look more elegant. Beautiful silver candlesticks stood among gold plates and silver utensils. Six antique wooden Louis XIII chairs upholstered in soft red velvet surrounded the table, their dark brown color matching the table and wood parquet. A French melody from the 1880s softly wafted from somewhere, completing the romantic, festive, and laid-back atmosphere.

Amandine and Lea walked up to the table and nodded with approval.

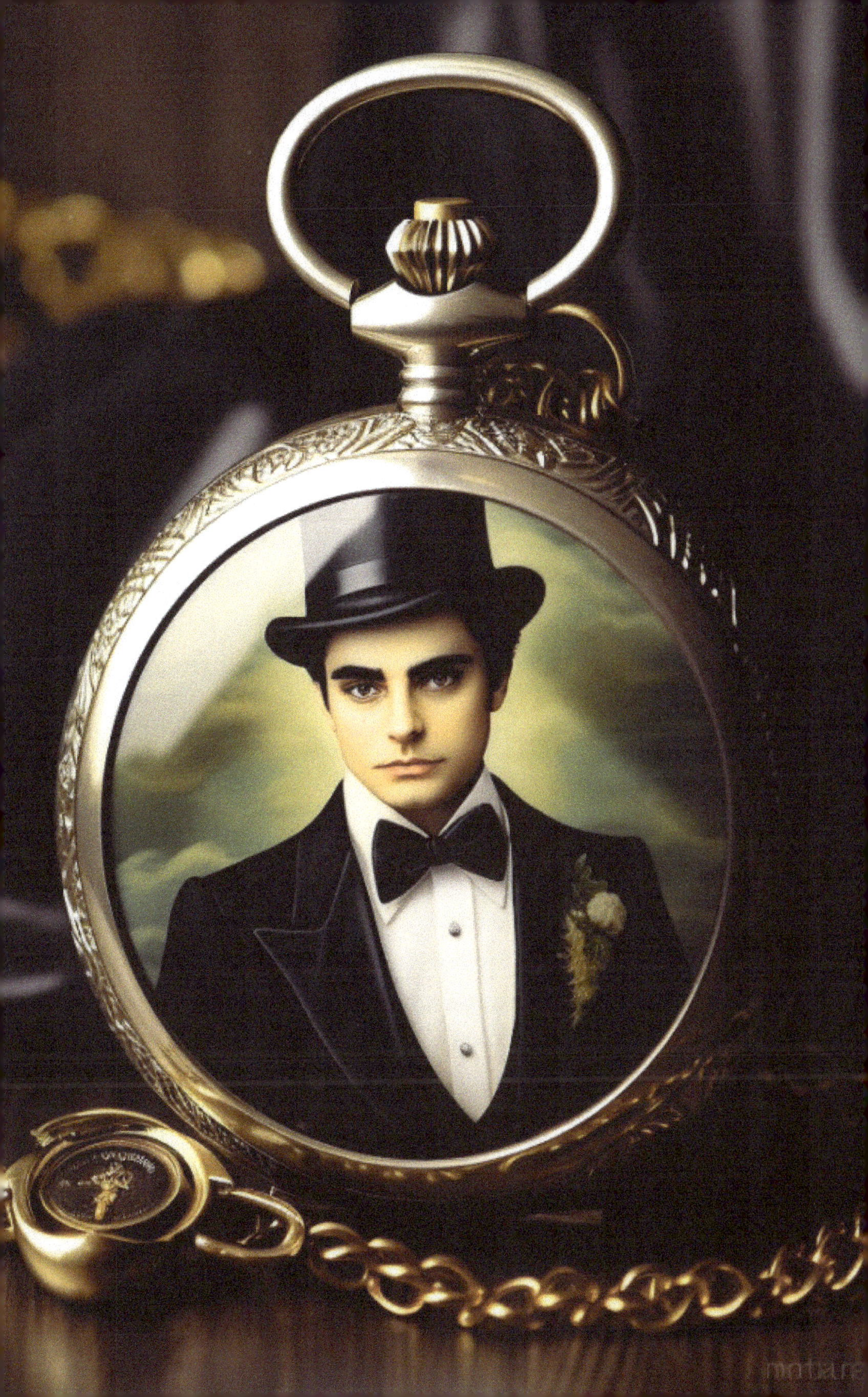

"It's pecking time!" Amandine winked her left eye at Lea. As soon as she spoke, Basil and Leon walked in through an invisible door trimmed with shimmering lights.

"Well, well, well, looks like someone was having a dreadful time at home!" Said Leon ironically and added, "He will be delighted!"

"I guess I shall dress for the occasion as well," said Basil, looking at Amandine.

He turned into a handsome young man with short black hair and attractive, bright features that gave his face bravery and kindness. His light hazel eyes simultaneously radiated with courage, daring, and irony. He smiled at everyone and gave his watching crowd a twirl. He wore the same stylish tuxedo with a black top hat, except his shoes were white and black patent leather, and his bow tie was black. His friends applauded with laughter.

"Indeed, an entrance to remember!" said Leon through the laughter.

A knock came at the door in the hallway, and a red-haired man with a mustache and beard entered the house with a warm smile. Leon met the guest in the hallway and hugged his old friend. Everyone followed Leon into the hallway to hug and greet the Artist. His eyes lit up with happiness from such a loving welcome from his dearest friends.

He spread his arms in amazement when he saw the beautiful feast. Amandine seated the Artist at the head of the table, and they all took their seats nearby.

It might seem strange and even unthinkable to the Grayville locals, but the friends began to dine sometime past seven in the evening.

# Chapter 9

# The Artist

*Every artist has to go through a lifelong journey to learn how to convey a vision of a muse on a canvas. However, one must live thousands of lives to learn how to create magic.*

*The Artist's Personal Journal*

*Every ending has its beginning, but not every beginning has its ending.*

*The Great Big Book of Contradictions and the Minds Generating Them*

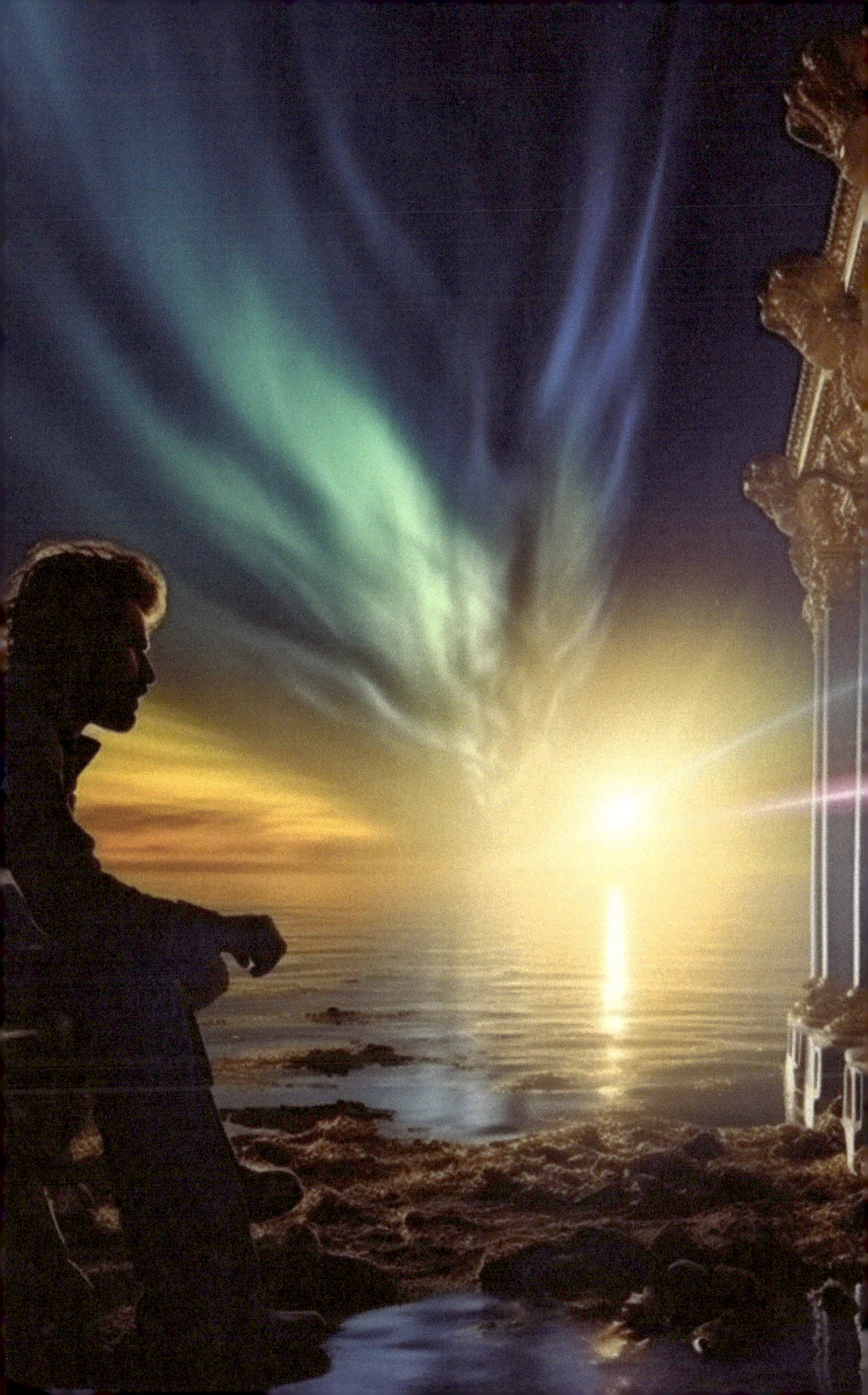

Perhaps not a single person in the world could boast of a collection of paintings as large as the one exhibited in the gallery of the Artist. Each image was alive and had its own story. The gallery occupied a vast hall full of light and warmth, with white columns covered in gold inlay. A luminescent stream of untraceable origin was everywhere, as if it were born out of and flowing into nowhere.

The Artist walked down the hallway, his footsteps echoing until he stopped by one of the paintings. The painting was strange; it looked more like a canvas with sketches, and gray tones prevailed exceptionally. He stared at the artwork for quite some time, imagining what could be changed.

Suddenly, he spoke. "Oh, no, I am late! My friends are expecting me for dinner."

With these words, he disappeared, within a fraction of a second.

# Chapter 10

# The Antiqua Bibliotheca

*Nothing in the world is ever completely wrong... Even a stopped clock is right twice a day.*

Paulo Coelho, *Brida*

A loud snap broke the silence. A colossal door creaked open, shedding dim light into a spacious room of the Antiqua Bibliotheca. No one had entered here for thousands of years. Spiderwebs and thick layers of dust covered the long rows of large bookshelves. To prepare the Bibliotheca for its first visitor in a long while, five cleaner drones flew inside, polished the entire premises in a minute, and then quickly flew out, softly buzzing like bumblebees.

A huge shadow appeared on the floor in the doorway, followed by tiny footsteps. The size of the creature didn't match the size of its shadow. As the footsteps continued getting closer to the room, the shadow diminished until it shrank to the child-like size of the creature who cast it. The shadow's owner was short, with a big head and small arms and legs. As it approached the doorway, sensors scanned it from head to toe with a red light, and a pleasant voice welcomed it. "Please enter."

The small creature walked in, and the door automatically closed behind it. Crystal chandeliers hung from the high ceiling on long golden chains, illuminated the library. Tall bookshelves stretched along the walls of the quiet, spacious room, which was adorned with parquet flooring. A long red carpet ran over the floor from the front door to the opposite wall, with a long reading table on top. One throne-like chair faced the door at the head of the table. Its high seat and tall back looked royally ceremonial.

The little creature walked majestically down the red carpet toward the table with a serious, pensive look. He was only a half-meter in height and had olive-colored skin and short limbs. His hair was sparse and short. The creature's big nose had a hump right in the middle. He had one set of ears and a pair of red-brown eyes. He wore a gray leather suit with a white shirt and black patent-leather shoes. An olive-colored silk tie and handkerchief made him look even more important.

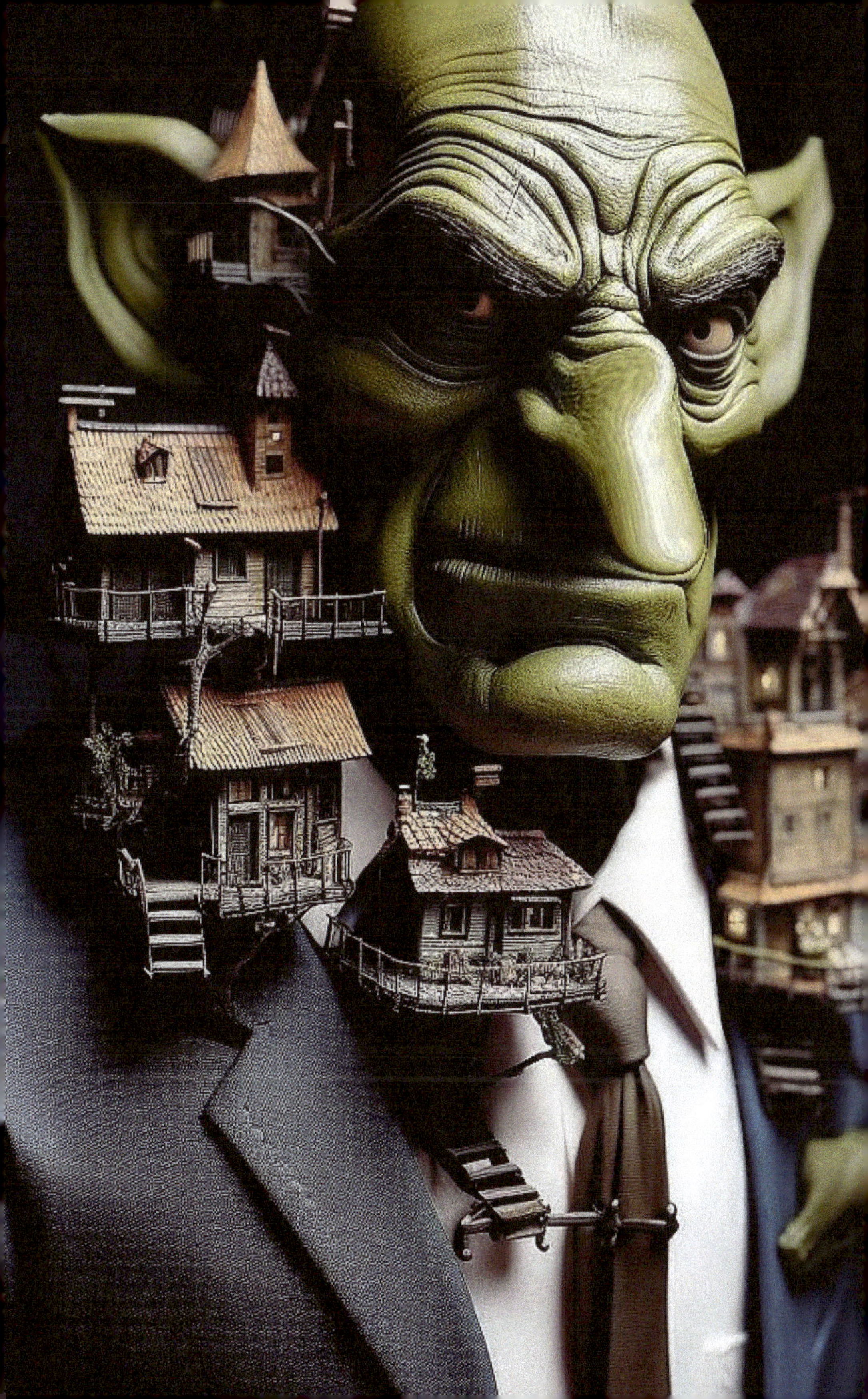

He got comfortable on the chair and sat like a king on a throne. His little legs dangled. He took a huge pipe out of his tiny pocket, inhaled a very long puff, held his breath momentarily, and released a toroidal cloud of smoke. The question of how the huge pipe fit in his tiny pocket remained unanswered. After a few minutes, he spoke in a squeaky voice, as if imitating someone's speech.

"The Greatest Councilor of the Council of the Ancients, Lord Grayus! We know nothing of those shiny spheres or the whereabouts of their existence!"

In response, he spoke calmly, in a deep, menacing voice.

"What if I were to insert you in the molecular press? Would that help you find the much-needed information?"

Again, he mimicked groveling.

"We are begging you, please don't do it! We will put forth all our efforts and exercise all available methods to trace them!"

"Fie!" Grayus indignantly spat on the floor.

A small cleaner robot appeared out of nowhere and quickly sucked in the fallen saliva with a mechanical proboscis. A melody played quietly, indicating the successful completion of the task, and the robot went about its business.

Grayus put a black glove on his right hand and pointed to the bookshelves. A book flew up to him. He quickly looked through several books in this manner, reading their names out loud and then sending them flying back to their shelves with another wave of his gloved hand.

"*Swift-Footed Tail's Hop: Feeding and Keeping in Captivity.* Not this one! *Paddle-Butt Parnovigana and Limb-Armed Maw: Crossbreeding and Breeding at Home.* Aggrr! Again, a waste of my time. *Human-Dolls' Wehrmacht: Reality or Myth.* No, no, aaaand nooo!" the big-nosed creature exclaimed, continuing his search.

"*Mind and Behavior Manipulations of Two-Legged Human-Dolls, Second Edition.* Stupid human-dolls! Not the right book, again! *Human-Doll Hunting: Baits, Lures, and Other Traps.* Damned human-dolls, little shits! What's next? *Gray-Farms of Human-Dolls: How to Get Maximum Doll-Coins With Minimal Investment.*" He growled and continued his quest for the right book.

"*The Main Rebellion of Human-Dolls and Its Suppression: The Greatest Commanders of Grayovius.* Oh, the massive battle in one of the gray-farm towns! My great-grandfather Grayovnus forever weaned human-dolls from love, fun, creativity, sympathy, compassion, affection and other atrocities... Aha-haha!" Grayus continued his search with laughter.

"*Human-Dolls as the Main Sources of Nutrition: Ideal Diet for Multi-Centennials.*" Suddenly, he laughed out loud.

"Ahahahaha, yeah, ideal. All I can remember is the huge belly of my uncle, Dumbpauncher. I'd rather be a bristle-snout piggy-grunt than eat human-dolls. My nose up their butts! Ahahahaha!"

Having laughed to his heart's content, he took a substantial booger out of his nose and threw it on the floor. The small cleaner robot again appeared and quickly sucked it up. After playing the quiet melody, the robot continued its other cleaning duties.

"*The Secret Treaty of Human-Dolls' Chiefs and the Shmyg Council of the Ancients of Grayovius: How to Extend the Lives of Human-Dolls and Preserve a Gray-Farm.* Ahh! No, again."

He summoned the next book.

"*Mages, Wizards, and Other Creatures of Chaos and How to Fight Them.* I found it! Finally! I swear by the Solemn Oath of the Shmygs, I will win this battle! For the glory of my favorite great-grandfather, Grayovnus!"

He joyfully exclaimed, taking the big book and jumping off the chair. As soon as he touched the floor, he slipped and fell with a rumble, dropping the book, which hit the floor with an even louder boom. Something fell out of it with a clang. As he approached it, he saw a gold key and picked it up. The top of the key was shaped like his family coat of arms: the doll-coin with crossed tailslavk and uporotnick leaves. The blade of the key was engraved in the language of the ancients.

The barely visible inscription read, *"See the visible, know the well-known, open the unlocked."*

"Stupid nonsense! Never mind, I will figure it out later."

Grayus put the key in his pocket, full of hope for future accomplishments. He took the massive book in his hands. He was sure his goodness and virtue—traits known to the rest of us as scheming and cunning—would win the day. He scampered out of the library into his study, nearly winded by the sheer effort of carrying a big book.

# Chapter 11

# The Shmygs

*The most potent weapon in the hands of the oppressor is the mind of the oppressed.*

Steve Biko

Beneath the Earth's surface, in depths where no human had ever set foot, there existed a secret species known as the shmygs. Petite in size, these beings typically measured a mere fifty centimeters tall. Yet scattered among their ranks were extraordinary giants who reached a full meter in height. Their skin was an olive color, and it was as resilient as armor.

Enormous cities built by these creatures spanned the entire subterranean layer of the Earth. Though their society reflected a human-like organization, the shmygs surpassed people with their advanced technological and scientific prowess. The shmygs called humans "dolls" because of the unique ability to bend human consciousness to their will using sophisticated devices. The dolls who were manipulated retained no memory of their actions, only what the shmygs chose to imprint in their minds.

Takeball was the shmygs' sport of choice, a game known for its brutality. It bore a strong resemblance to baseball, yet differed in that the ball used was significantly heavier, and the game was played at much higher speeds. Mistakes were common and frequently resulted in severe injuries to the players. Betting offices thrived on this danger, offering wagers exclusively on the injuries incurred—ranging from various types of fractures and dislocations to limb loss, concussions, and cranial traumas.

The shmygs were master manipulators who primarily used humans to harvest their world's unique currency, the doll-coin. In order to earn a single doll-coin, the shmygs had to ensure that their human-dolls adhered strictly to a specific algorithm before and during their sleep. Human-doll dreams were the source of this currency, and expert shmyg manipulators closely monitored the delicate process. The quality of the dream was crucial; only when a human-doll experienced a pleasant dream did it yield a doll-coin, making the shmygs' nocturnal task both critical and intricate.

The control over humans served more than just economic gain; it was also a form of entertainment. The shmygs could commandeer any person to indulge in acts that were not permissible in Grayovius, the vast world where the shmygs resided.

Grayovius was a sprawling network of thousands of cities teeming with factories, workshops, commerce and leisure spots, research labs, centers of learning, doll-coin farms, health facilities, tobacco farms, water systems, and a myriad of other residential and administrative constructions. The shmygs' world also boasted subterranean resorts complete with artificial suns and water features. These were so lifelike one could scarcely believe they were nestled deep in the Earth's crust, a stone's throw from the core. The ingenuity of the shmygs' transportation system enabled them to move quickly underground. The shmygs could zip across their domain in mere minutes, thanks to their network of high-speed pneumatic capsules.

Governance in Grayovius was firmly in the hands of The Shmygs Council Of The Ancients, whose decrees were followed without question. Their society was equipped with police, judiciary, and other branches of governance. The secret police, however, was particularly notable. They wielded significant power to execute the Council's clandestine directives and maintained peace in Grayovius.

The shmyg population was divided into clans that frequently clashed over the coveted right to control dolls. It had been many millennia since the last Great Underground War. In its aftermath, a peace treaty was enacted to prohibit military actions within Grayovius; clans now resolved their disputes using dolls. Above ground, humanity was embroiled in incessant armed conflicts, wars, and brawls, oblivious to the fact that they were merely pawns in the shmygs' intricate clan conflicts.

Humans, by nature, were not prone to violence; they wouldn't hurt a fly on their own. But under a manipulator's influence, they could transform into deadly weapons, wreaking havoc indiscriminately. A person who wandered the streets in peace was probably not under manipulation and posed no threat to others. Yet there were numerous instances where a person, previously gentle and stable, inexplicably committed a heinous act against their family and themselves. Such drastic changes in behavior often pointed to shmygs' manipulation.

The reasons a manipulator targeted someone varied widely; it could be a personal vendetta, a bad day, or just a whim. Regardless, with the human population having surged to eight billion, such incidents were overlooked, particularly as the Council contemplated culling the numbers by design.

Deadly diseases did not just randomly appear on Earth's surface. They were the product of the shmygs' laboratories, where kidnapped human-dolls endured terrifying experiments. Under directives from the Administration for the Regulation of Doll Population (ARDP), an array of lethal viruses was engineered.

Once the doll population reached the desired levels, those viruses would be remotely neutralized by technicians using specialized data transmission channels. In the shmygs' labs, they developed not only viruses but also medicines, which were covertly dispensed through the water supply systems during unexpected epidemics in the human-doll world.

The shmygs often released their captives from the laboratories after they had been kidnapped, but only after altering their memories of the events. Some victims retained no memories, while others were left with implanted recollections of alien abductions, complete with detailed accounts of spacecraft and green extraterrestrials with oversized heads and eyes. These memories were as vivid as the psycho-correctors' imagination permitted, the professionals tasked with memory modification. Typically, these shmyg scientists held several advanced degrees, with a comprehensive course in Gestalt phycology being a requisite part of their education.

Unlike humans, shmygs never fell ill in the way humans comprehended sickness. Yet, they were vulnerable to a very rare and lethal disease known as shumiha. The condition began with a faint noise in the ears that slowly escalated into an excruciating din. It was a fearsome affliction, non-contagious and infrequent. Its causes remaining a mystery. On the whole, shmygs outlived humans for centuries. The average male lived for 2,500 years, while the average female lived for 3,000. This longevity was partly explained by the fact that pregnant female shmygs would enter a deep hibernation for about three hundred years to allow their offspring to develop. Physiologically, a female could only bear children up to four times, as her body required roughly three hundred years to recuperate after each birth.

    Childbirth among the shmygs was always an extraordinary event. As the moment arrived, the newborn would independently make its way out of the womb, sever its own umbilical cord, carry out the necessary disinfection, and only then rouse its mother. Remarkably sensible from the moment of birth, the infant engaged in lengthy discussions with its mother about its future role in shmyg society, sharing its inherent talents, abilities, and inclinations. The mother, in turn, made the call on the child's destiny and the profession it would pursue.

    Upon the child's arrival, the father would invariably endorse the decisions made by his spouse and the infant. Historical records of the shmygs mention only one father who ever contested the mother's choice. Legend has it that he was immediately afflicted by shumiha and succumbed to excruciating torment.

    Consequently, no one has since dared to challenge the opinion of a shmyg mother and risk suffering such a grim fate.

Everything in life was relative. Shmygs manipulated human-dolls, who were completely oblivious to the manipulation and shmygs' existence. In turn, shmygs were also unaware of the universe's vigilant eyes that watched over all that occurred on Earth and throughout space. These observant beings, known as the guardians, carried the vital mission of maintaining balance and harmony within the boundless stretches of the Morpho Amathonte galaxy.

# Chapter 12

# The Mill

*The balanced feeding of human-dolls significantly increases a gray-farm's service life and profitability.*

*Gray-Farms of Human-Dolls:
How to Get Maximum Doll-Coins
With Minimal Investment*

Rebis Millis had lived for almost fifty years. He could not remember anything but his gray house and the mill behind it all his life. It seemed to him that he had known all the ins and outs of milling work since he was born.

Every day of his life went according to a tight schedule. After waking and freshening up in the bathroom, he dressed and had breakfast. Then, he fed and tended to the horses, harnessed the cart, and made his way two miles to the Graynson's farm. He picked up four grain bags, took them back to the mill, ground them into flour, poured them into two bags, and took them to two bakeries in town, one at the beginning and the other in the middle of Gray Street.

Nothing he did after finishing his work for the day was important. He could not make sense of anything besides the millwork. He never remembered what he had done in his free time the day before.

However, he vividly remembered one unpleasant event about a week ago that had happened to him, or rather to the mill. On that ill-fated day, the water wheel suddenly jammed. He barely heard a small knock, but it was as if a loud siren went off in his head. He rushed to the mill, only having time to put on his underpants. He found a considerable log in the water wheel. It weighed about 200 pounds, and had damaged a couple of blades and locked the rotation mechanism. He picked up the log as if it were mere fluff, pulled it out of the wheel, and dropped it nearby. Rebis replaced the blades and opened the dam's partition. The mill worked again as if nothing had happened, and he was pleased.

He sat down on the log, then got up and stared at the unwitting culprit of the incident for a long time, trying to make sense of it. He tried to lift it, but it was now so heavy he could barely move it. He let go, and it fell back into position with a din.

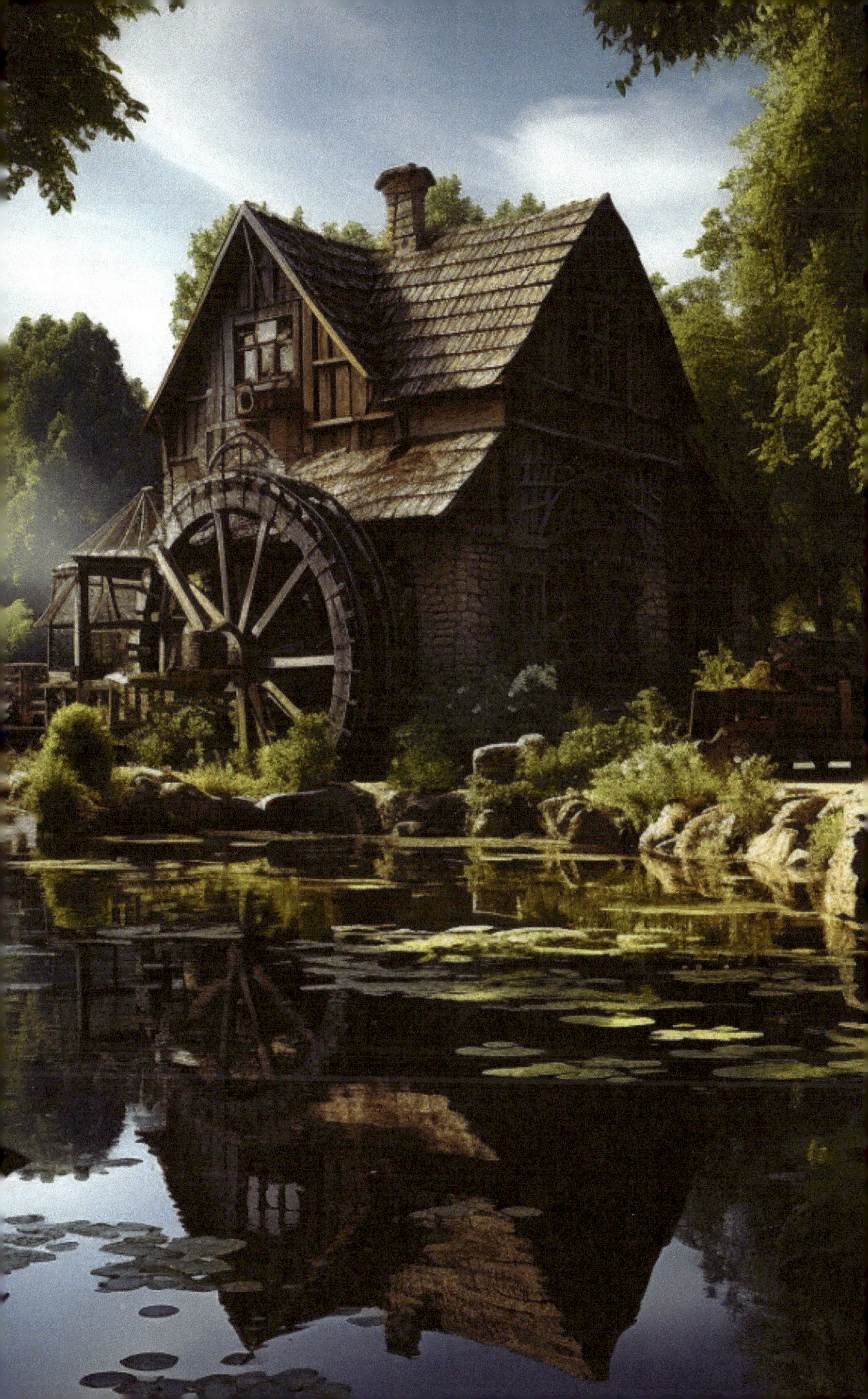

The bewildering incident firmly stuck in his mind, a key event in his life. His memory clung greedily to it, hinting to Rebis that the true beauty of life was in the randomness of events that could happen, good and bad, funny and sad, joyful and regretful. But whenever he tried to think further on that idea, it quickly faded away, swallowed by the gray shroud of days. Nothing could disturb his iron schedule and his gray hopelessness. He would always remain a miller, for whom a tight schedule was of utmost importance.

# Chapter 13

# The Miner

*The dreams of human-dolls are precious sources of doll-coins, as their thoughts are free, bright, and boundless during sleep. Enhancing diet and living conditions in a gray-farm allows for optimal harvesting conditions, making doll-coin mining even more successful.*

*Mind and Behavior Manipulation of Two-Legged Human-Dolls, Second Edition*

In his early youth, at about five hundred years old, Grayus was intrigued by establishing his own gray-farm. Mining was an attribute of nobility in his surroundings, not only because it was profitable but also because it was humane from a shmyg point of view.

Human-dolls simply wasted a huge part of their lives. They spent their days in senseless drunkenness, revelry, and debauchery. They fell in love and had fun, cried, swore, killed, and maimed each other.

For example, the well-known human-dolls' Wehrmacht came at a significant cost. It happened when one male human-doll decided to burn a whole human-doll nation's population in furnaces. Other human-dolls fought him bravely and won in the end. However, the loss of shmyg-miners in that war was tremendous and deplorable. Thousands and thousands of gray-farms were lost, but millions and millions of human-dolls had no clue that those ideas of senseless existence came to them through their dreams while they were asleep.

One human-doll, who worked at a regular human-doll bureau in Grayus' first gray-farm, was unaware that he was part of a vast gray-farm system. He was programmed with a simple algorithm: wake up, go to the bathroom, wash up, get dressed, have breakfast, come to work, make deals following the strategy written in his memory, finish the job, and come home. Afterward, he did senseless activities.

However, he somehow managed to disturb the algorithm, which in turn could have jeopardized the existence of the entire production chain of the whole gray-farm. All of that happened because of one attractive female human-doll who moved into an apartment close to his. Every day, she met him after work and tried to talk to him to start a relationship.

In two weeks, partly due to the supervising manipulator's negligence, she broke through his mind and planted love in him, and he began to have erotic dreams about her. The incident broke all the communication between the assembly module and the control module of the mind manipulation, which triggered algorithmic errors that caused him to make bad deals for the bureau.

Grayus demoted him by programming him with an absolute passion and adoration for pottery. The human-doll quit willingly and got a job as a pottery maker at a small boutique pottery shop near his home.

It was very funny, especially since another human-doll had been eyeing his position at the bureau for a long time. Grayus' intervention helped to avoid a ruinous production collapse at the gray-farm. Eventually, the new human-doll was upgraded to another program at the bureau without any problems, went through synchronization, and worked like clockwork.

There was no need even to change the schedule hanging on his wall. He followed it diligently. Grayus let him buy a big house and earn millions in human-doll money as a reward.

The big-nosed shmyg was happy with the outcome, and his conscience was clear. He extended the human-dolls' lives by caring for their health through a balanced, nutritious diet and enforcing a strict regimen of work and sleep, during which their dreams were observed and turned into doll-coins.

All human-dolls were programmed with algorithms tailored to their daily activities. Grayus required very little in return—just one doll-coin per day from each naive human-doll bug.

# Chapter 14

# Shmygus Superiors

*The creation of "new" shmygs is a massive step for us. I believe this breakthrough will benefit every shmyg for generations to come.*

Research notes of the "old" shmyg,<br>Dr. Shterust Proherst

The shmygs were pedantic, law-abiding, intelligent, thrifty, inventive, tactical, strict, and responsible. Believing they had the world's best interests at heart with their human-dolls, their most defining trait was an unyielding obsession with order and micromanaging every facet of their lives.

Tens of thousands of years ago in human-doll time, or a few generations ago for shmygs, these completely unemotional beings derived a formula for a very complex genetic code of shmygs. This led to the formation of shmyg genetic engineering. The fundamental discovery was presented to The Shmyg Council Of The Ancients. The secret agenda of the Council had always been to create a superior race of shmygs.

After extensive genetic engineering research, The Shmyg Council Of The Ancients authorized a secret operation named "Shmygus Superiors" to create two heterosexual "new" shmygs. This major evolutionary breakthrough eventually led to the formation of caste communities. The shmygs of smaller height, about fifty centimeters, were from the highest caste and held the highest posts in Grayovius. The shmygs of taller height, about a meter high, were considered giants and were from the lowest castes.

The Shmyg Council Of The Ancients and The Great Counselor at the time, Lord Grayovnus, thoroughly watched the "new" couple. They were the smartest of all the shmygs and passed all the tests with the highest marks. At the same time, their genetic code included an imprint of respect and honor to the shmygs' customs and traditions. The desire to pursue the extermination of "old" shmygs was removed from their genetic code, to prevent them from becoming proud and attempting their destruction.

This major evolutionary breakthrough led to The Shmyg Council Of The Ancients' endorsement of an important scientific and social bill: Secretious

Castous. The bill included a prerequisite for all shmygs to be placed into different caste communities.

While only the shmygs with superior verbal, visual, auditory, physical, and mental abilities could belong to the highest caste, they also had to be considered the most beautiful shmygs in Grayovius. These shmygs were the smallest in height, approximately half a meter.

Some males had large noses characterized by humps in the middle, which served as a testament to the nobility of their bloodline. These noble shmygs also had very large heads.

No females exceeded sixty centimeters in height, and they had disproportionately large heads compared to their small bodies. However, their noses were different: they resembled half of a round bun, which made them appear cheerful and attractive to male shmygs.

Due to their height, all female shmygs automatically belonged to the highest caste. If the family of a female shmyg lacked the funds to maintain her status, she had to be given to a wealthier family. If a male from a lower caste wished to marry a female shmyg, he would have to woo her for five hundred years in a manner she deemed fit. The female shmygs were highly intelligent, perceptive, witty, and communicative. Therefore, they played important roles in the life of Grayovius. Last but not least, as charming as they were, females were always responsible for bringing harmony throughout all of Grayovius, the entire land of shmygs.

The Great Councillor Lord Grayovnus and the Shmyg Council of the Ancients were very pleased with the population of "new" shmygs. They had decided to begin integrating them slowly into the community. The leaders of Grayovius concluded that no one should know about the "Shmygus Superiors" operation to avoid any confusion and unrest among "old" shmygs.

As a result, all knowledge about the secret operation to create the "new" shmygs was placed in a hyper-her-metically sealed safe that could guard the information for a long-long time. The "old" shmygs who participated in the secret operation were rewarded with the highest honor: they were imprinted in the annals of shmyg history as creators. Together with their families and the safe, the creators were hidden in secret, remote caves and given orders to guard all information about "Shmygus Superiors."

The safe had an interesting attribute; it was designed only to be opened with one specific key. The keeper of the key was the only shmyg who knew about the location of the secret caves. It was the Great Councillor Lord Grayovnus, the favorite great-grandfather of Grayus.

# Chapter 15

# The Underground

*Imma tell you this, bud: the human-doll dreams can be unpredictably intricate and even crazy. However, if a nightmare enters their stupid brain, watch yo back...*

Shift Supervisor of the Collection,<br>Filtration, and Dream-Processing Plant

Perhaps one of the most significant achievements of shmyg ingenuity was the invention of hipper-absorbers and mega-converters that turned human-dolls' dreams into doll-coins. Shmyg manipulators placed hipper-absorbers into the brains of human-dolls everywhere. Once the shmygs gained control over humanity, they established their reign on Earth and initiated the mining of doll-coins worldwide.

From one valid dream of a human-doll, they made one doll-coin. Of course, the main purpose of the innovation was exceptionally self-serving and focused on automating the absorption, analysis, processing, and conversion of human-doll dreams to doll-coins. Properly scaling this process resulted in multiplied production and, in turn, increased the profit growth rate for shmyg-miners' gray-farms. In the shortest possible time, deep underground in places not accessible to human-dolls, all shmyg living territories were shrouded with ingenious, cobweb-like plexuses of dream-collecting pipes equipped with various filters, accelerators, retarders, splitters, and enrichers. Thousands of plants collected, filtered, and processed the raw dream material. This enriched dream material was transferred to other plants for conversion to doll-coins.

The most intelligent shmygs from the highest caste, the crème de la crème, worked at the conversion plants as directors, plant managers, manipulators, engineers, analysts, distributors, financiers, and counting commissioners.

At the opposite end of the spectrum, at the collection, filtration, and processing plants, regular shmygs from the lowest castes made incredible efforts and risked their lives daily.

The biggest rewards they could count on in their careers for their hard, dangerous work were promotions to a shift supervisor positions and, possibly, the Honorable Shmyg Medal, if the plant manager would approve the application. However, even the

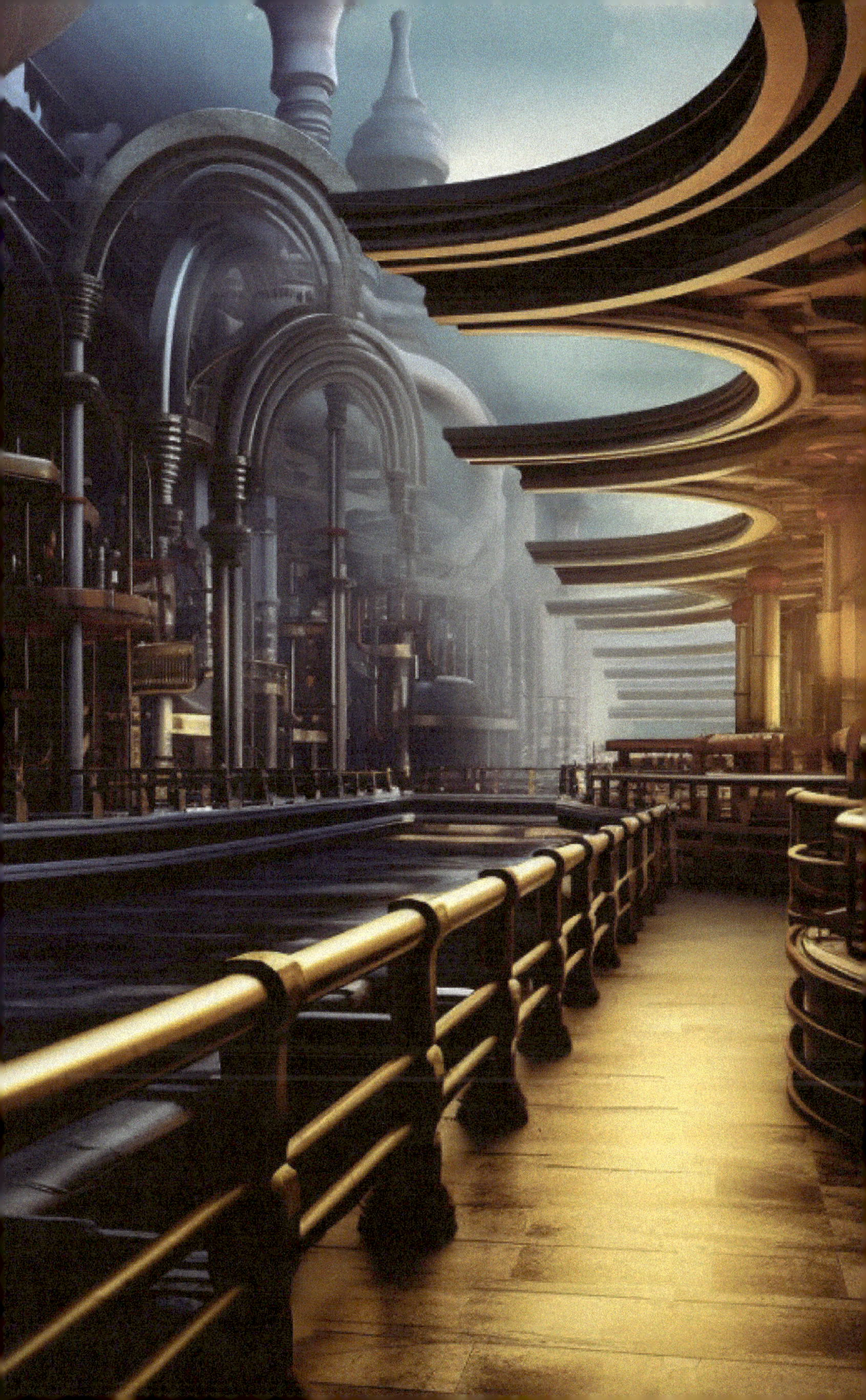

prospect of becoming the shift supervisor was highly appealing to them, as it meant a substantial salary increase, a guarantee of safe work, and complete respect from other employees. Those dedicated dungeon workers had no idea of the amount of work the high-caste manipulators, engineers, curators, architects, designers, and builders did before them. All that hard work was done to ensure the delivery of processed and enriched final dream material to the conversion plants.

They had no need to know all that information. One of their many tasks included catching anomalous chunks of dream mass formed due to human-doll nightmares, which happened on rare occasions due to non-compliance with their diet.

These incidents warranted a thorough internal investigation by the plant manager; more often than not, nightmares occurred due to the negligence of the curating shmyg manipulator. Later, if his guilt were proven, the poor fellow was subjected to a terrible public execution.

The execution would usually be carried out in the plant endangered by the crime. The shmyg judge would declare the verdict over a loudspeaker when workers gathered in the central room for announcements. The culprit would not be allowed last words. The Grayovius anthem would play, the unfortunate shmyg would be placed in a press for processing dream waste, and a shift supervisor would

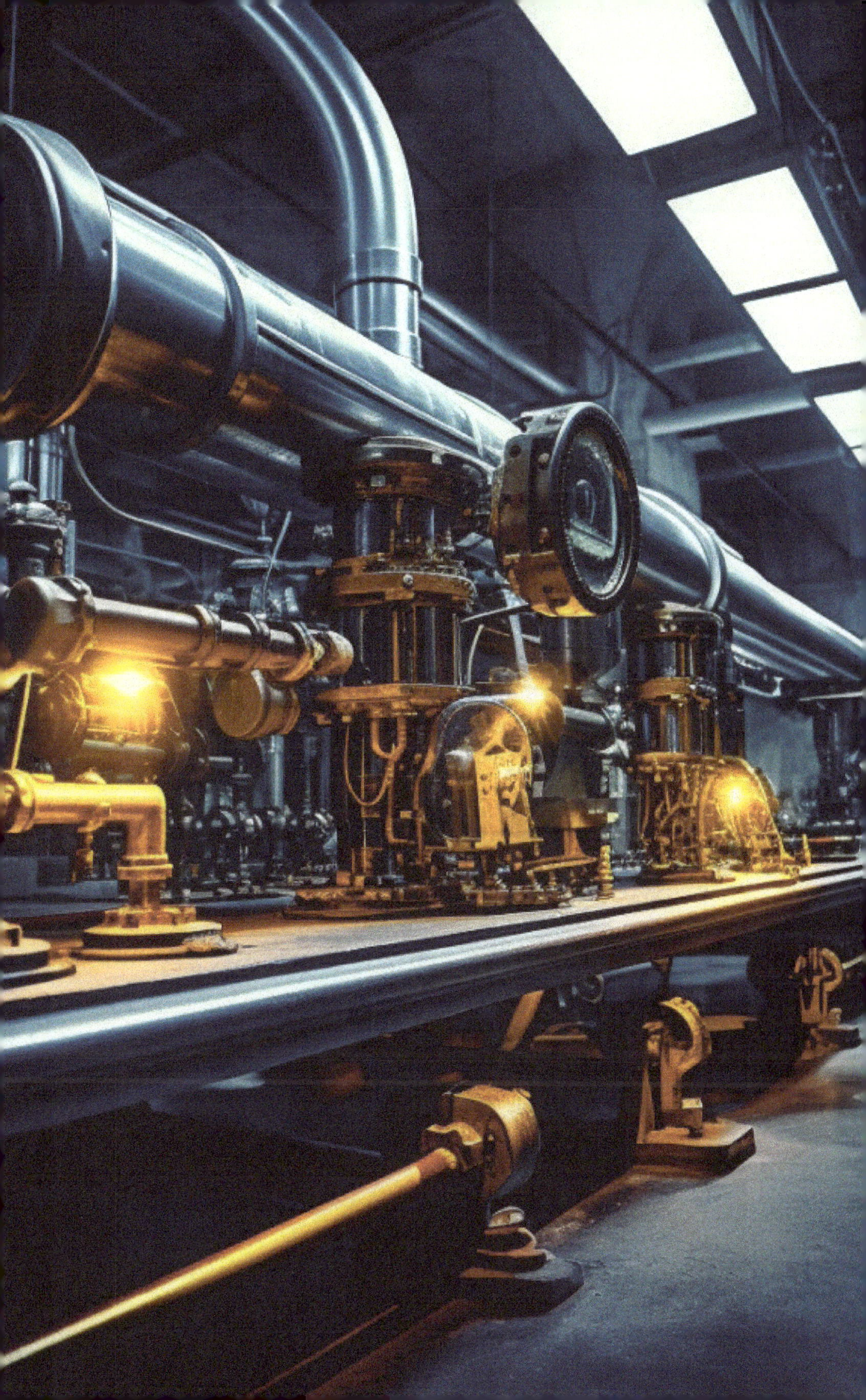

press the button. After a couple of seconds, the dream waste and the culprit with it would be turned into a pink clot of matter, approximately the size of an ice cube. It would slowly evaporate into the air, leaving behind a pleasant floral smell. Afterward, everyone would diverge to their posts and immediately return to performing their daily duties as if nothing had happened.

Among the workers, there was a special task force of trappers, who manually caught anomalous pieces of dream mass. These slick, athletic fellow shmygs had to pass a special selection process and possess the highest moral qualities, such as courage, bravery, and a strong spirit. For them, there was no greater honor than death from catching an abnormal dream mass chunk, which came from human-doll nightmares at an incredible speed.

In a catastrophic accident in the Koreansk Plateau area, an abnormal chunk of dream mass accelerated to a speed of over 1,300 miles per hour. It smashed an emergency braking system into chips, pierced through three well-equipped elite trappers, and penetrated four especially strong barrier plates. Uncontrolled, it transferred most of its accumulated kinetic energy to the ground, causing a powerful underground explosion. The blowup not only destroyed the entire communication department and the poor shmygs within a seventy-mile radius, but also caused a devastating earthquake on the surface of the earth, along with a tsunami of more than twenty meters high. Thousands of human-dolls and tens of thousands of shmygs died. The human-dolls called the strongest earthquake in history the Great Chilean Earthquake, and the shmygs called it Rara Hyperkinetic Visio Nocturne, which translates to Rare Hyperkinetic Night Vision.

That incident catalyzed changes to security and approval of a new system: the Official Classifier of Human-Doll Nightmares, with gradation depending on longevity, complexity, and destructive power. If the nightmare lasted two minutes, it was called a double, three minutes, a triple, four, a quadro, five, a pento. If the nightmare lasted more than six minutes, the human-doll's hyper-observer was temporarily disconnected from the system to prevent civilian casualties.

# Chapter 16

# Tiberius

*Through every generation of the human race there has been a constant war, a war with fear. Those who have the courage to conquer it are made free and those who are conquered by it are made to suffer until they have the courage to defeat it.*

Alexander The Great

*I think there's no question about who actually invented baseball.*

Director of Sport, GBC
(Grayovius Broadcasting Company)

A warm artificial light flowed from the window of the locker room, illuminating the powerful silhouette of the shmyg. He was at least a meter high. It was about ten minutes before the start of the final game of the season, and the stands outside loudly chanted his name. The champion's emotionless face, clean and calm like a glade on the shores of a lake, had a huge scar sprawling over it.

Born into the poor family of a simple shmyg worker, Tiberius followed in the footsteps of his father. From his childhood, he dreamed of becoming a trapper. Even after undergoing rigorous selection and testing, Tiberius became a trapper earlier than usual. His remarkable height and natural strength stood out among his peers. He had always been proud of his work; with ease and without injury, he caught doubles and even triples.

Tiberius would have remained an unknown trapper, but one day, a yellow signal lamp lit up over the discharge pipe's outlet at the plant for collection, filtration, and processing. A loud siren rang out inside the trapping department. Seven on-duty trappers put on gravitational gloves for catching an abnormal dream mass chunk and rushed to their places. Their large figures froze by the discharge pipe's outlet in nervous anticipation.

Tiberius was the fourth closest to the pipe. A barely discernible buzz gradually increased and grew so loud it seemed as if something huge was approaching them.

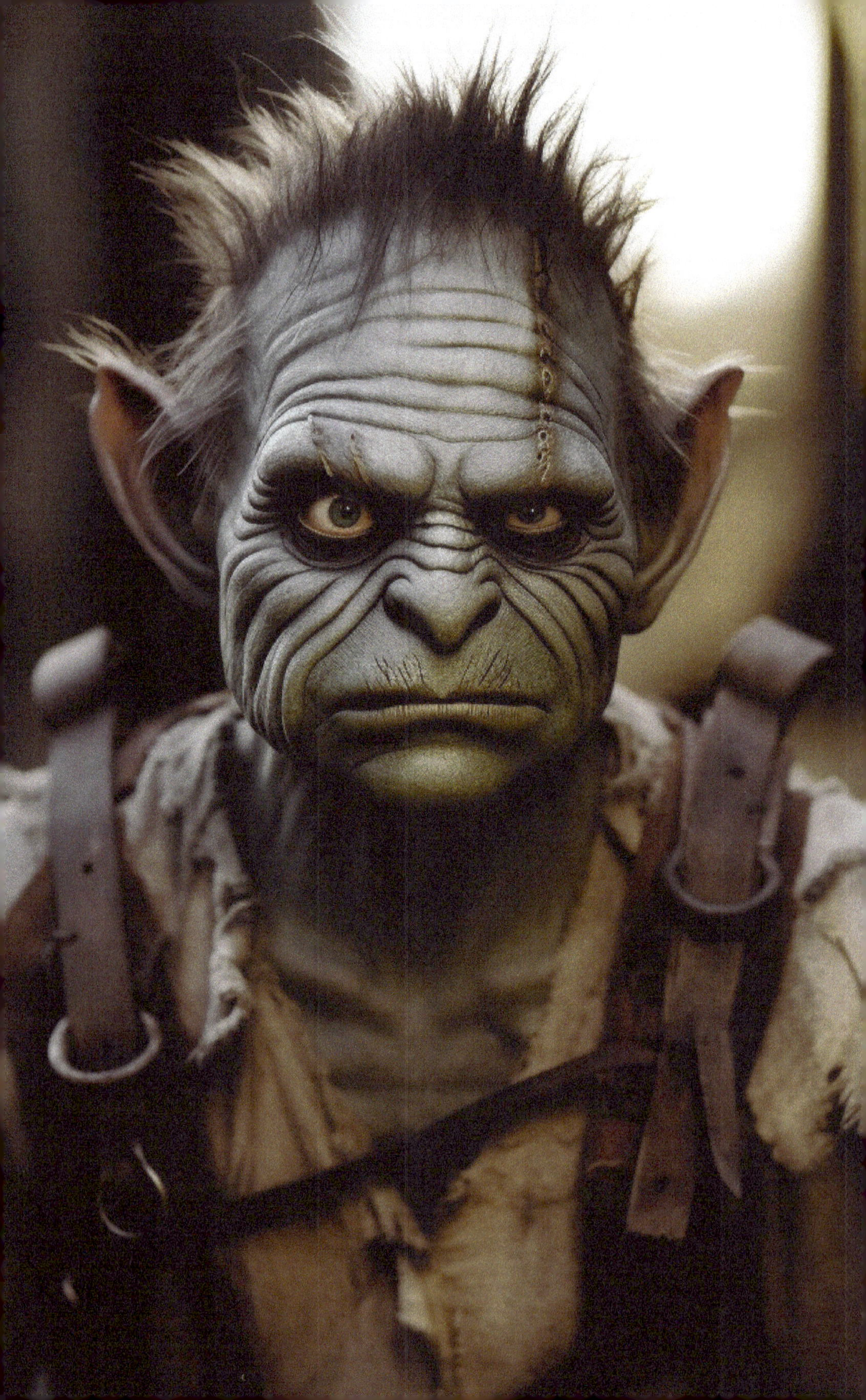

For a moment, they thought they were in a jar being shaken for fun by a giant.

When the buzz and vibrations became unusually powerful, the dream mass chunk flew out of the pipe at a speed of 400 miles per hour. It was a quadro.

In a split second, the abnormal dream mass chunk demolished the first trapper's head as if it had never been on his shoulders. The second trapper put up a glove and prepared to catch it, but this did not help him much; the quadro flew right through him. The third trapper prepared to catch the quadro, but the fate of the first two awaited him.

Tiberius saw it in slow motion. He quickly crouched down and prepared for a sharp turn in the air. As soon as the abnormal dream mass chunk took the life of the third catcher, he sharply jumped up, setting his glove along the trajectory of the quadro.

An acute pain burned his face as it made contact with the quadro's gravitational field, but he continued his coup in the air. When the quadro flew into the glove, the glove's gravitational lock clamped onto it and flung Tiberius into the air, twisting him several times. The glove, still clutching the abnormal matter tightly, continued its journey, but without Tiberius, who flew out of the glove and right into the shift supervisor's booth. The glove scattered the three remaining trappers in different directions, akin to bowling pins. It dented the first compensation plate with a roar and then fell to the floor, swinging around its axis like a top.

Tiberius was the first trapper ever to survive an encounter with a quadro. The main supervisor himself visited him in the hospital and presented him with the Honorable Shmyg Medal.

Now, in the locker room, he focused on the upcoming game. He heard the audience begin to chant even louder as the host warmed up the crowd, announcing his name and listing all his titles. Tiberius headed to the field with quick, confident steps. When he entered the brightly lit stadium, hundreds of thousands of spectators buzzed with admiration and stood up from their seats, shouting his name. When the crowd settled down, he took his place as captain of the team of nine shmygs, and the anthem of Grayovius began to play.

# Chapter 17

# The Covert Operation

*Our sorrowful efforts shall not be in vain! The spark shall ignite into a flame, and our enlightened populace shall gather beneath the sacred banner.*

Shpik Chubatius's Personal Journal

The small door of the safe house quickly opened. A half-meter shmyg wearing a hooded cloak rushed into the semi-dark room. It was Shpik Chubatius, the leader of the covert coup. Another shmyg of the same height immediately closed the door and joyfully and quietly greeted him. The guest threw off his hood, revealing a round head with sparse gray hair, then removed his cloak and handed it to the other shmyg, who graciously hung it on a hanger. He led the guest deep into a narrow corridor until they entered another room guarded by a meter-high shmyg thunderbolt guard.

Undercover leaders from different regions of Grayovius had already gathered, and sat around a circular table positioned at the center of the room. A low-hanging ceiling lamp brightly shone on the surface of the table, only slightly illuminating the faces of the covert shmygs. All had long awaited their chief's arrival while smoking their pipes.

When he entered the room, everyone rejoiced silently, unquestionably following the laws of conspiracy. The chief sat down on the chair specifically prepared for him, gathered his thoughts, and spoke in a quiet voice.

"Comgades!" He spoke with a burr, pronouncing Gs instead of Rs.

"Deag Comgades, shmygs! It's time for the tegible actions!" He said with a slight tapping on the floor with his leg.

"It's time to ovegthgow the highest caste—the basis of the Council of the Ancients of Ggayovius, which is sucking the blood out of shmyg-wogkegs!"

The shmygs quietly applauded. He gave them a slight wave with his hand, and the noise stopped.

Suddenly, the chief shmyg rose from the chair, laid his thumbs behind the edges of his waistcoat, and paced, looking directly at his feet.

Finally, he stopped in the middle of the room, proudly threw his head up, and continued his speech as if he were standing on an imaginary stage.

"Oug comgades' fist!" He squeezed his small fist threateningly. In the darkness, someone giggled, which made him realize that his fist looked comical and non-threatening. He then shifted into a different pose.

"Oug pgoud example of honog is the loyal comgade Tibegius and the hundgeds of thousands of faces he will lead! He will ggasp the gidge of the Council of the Ancients, once and fog all, and fgee the wogkegs fgom oppgession. Fagms and doll-coins to the wogking castes! Hoogay comgades!!!"

Everyone quietly inhaled the tobacco from their pipes, held their breath for a moment, slowly exhaled toroidal puffs of smoke, and let out a threefold hooray. They gathered more closely at the table to whisper about the details of the upcoming coup.

# Chapter 18

# The Manipulator

*It is strictly forbidden to create tyrants, terrorists, killers, and other similar destroyers in the gray-farm. If a violation is detected, notify the main supervisor immediately.*

Basic Gray-Farm Security Protocols

The door to an apartment swung open. Scared and breathing hard, Shpik ran inside and closed the door behind him. He waited, listening to the sounds coming from outside until he stopped hearing anything suspicious. He relaxed for a bit, sitting on a small chair and leaning back, exhaling with relief. Exciting thoughts grew in his head and prevented him from focusing on the traitor's identity.

"How and when did a Ggayovius Secget Segvice (GSS) agent, og agents, infiltgate the netwogk? Why did I succeed in caggying out the most ggandiose and bloodiest gevolution in the laggest empige of the human-dolls, and why didn't I succeed in doing the same hege in Ggayovius?"

Shpik remembered his mistakes even then. Intoxicated by power, he had not noticed the betrayal inside the gray-farm, the planned attempt by the turned party member. The plan failed, but it disrupted the mind of the human-dolls' revolutionary pseudo-leader. It had almost destroyed Shpik's plans to seize power over the whole empire. The bullet in the assassination attempt of the human-dolls' pseudo-leader was poisoned. The consciousness of the pseudo-leader he manipulated got infected with a disease of madness and stopped succumbing to manipulation. It made him very angry back then. He had been trying, in vain, to uncover the traitor when he arranged a real massacre at the farm. He subjugated a mustachioed human-doll and destroyed millions of human-dolls—counter-revolutionaries, so to speak—in retaliation.

He knew for sure the Grayovius secret police agents had uncovered seven out of ten clandestine locations. Even if the other three were beyond suspicion, it was only a matter of time. Agents would knock out all the necessary information from his associates through torture. The coverts only knew each other's operational pseudonyms, but many of them also knew each other's faces and the addresses of conspiratorial apartments. It was enough for the GSS to get everything in their claws—and get to him.

He approached the bookshelf, realizing that he might be seeing everything here for the last time. He picked up the Academy of Manipulation cup, which he was awarded three hundred years ago, as the best graduate. In his first years as a junior manipulator, work brought him only joy. He was a very self-motivated worker. After thirty years, he took a position as a senior manipulator. A hundred years of impeccable service to Grayovius flew by like one day. The acknowledgment board was hung with dozens of letters of gratitude, recognitions, and medals—and then he got bored.

He started experimenting with the human-dolls entrusted to him. The first time his unacceptable manipulations were discovered, he framed his colleagues, who then went under attack by the GSS agents. They didn't even have time to understand what had happened when they got inserted in the molecular press. **"When the fogest is chopped, the chips come flying,"** his father always said. Suddenly, there was a loud knock at the door. Calmly,

Shpik ran his palm over his head and opened it, relieved that everything would finally be over.

# Chapter 19

# Chubata

*In order to prevent the destruction of human-doll civilization, it is forbidden to organize global military games with their participation.*

Basic Gray-Farm Security Protocols

The knock repeated, and Shpik, slightly slowing, humbly opened the door of his small apartment. On the doorstep, accompanied by personal security, stood Grayus himself, smiling victoriously. Shpik stared at him with a terrified look, unsure of what to do next.

"According to the rules of etiquette, I think you, my kind friend, should invite me to come in," said Grayus with a cunning smirk.

"Yes, yes, of cougse, please come in. I'm soggy fog my sluggishness."

The until-recently almighty leader of the rebels shrank in front of Grayus.

Grayus signaled the guards to stay outside and stepped in. Meter-tall thunderbolt guards quickly closed the door behind him. Shpik moved to take Grayus's coat, but Grayus declined with a sloppy hand signal. Together, they went into a room, and Grayus immediately, without invitation, sat on the single chair as if it were a throne. He silently stared Shpik down with a sharp gaze for a long time, as though he were looking at a guilty schoolboy or studying some very rare specimen of an outlandish animal.

Finally, he took out a folder, put it on his knees, and slowly read out loud, starting with the cover.

"Personal file No.533ZHG/MA-978657. Senior Shmyg Manipulator of the tenth highest rank, Shpik Chubatius. Over 1,252 years of the genus. Growth 51.5 centimeters (average). Graduated with honors from the Academy of Manipulation. Owns the Passing Cup of the Academy to this day. He was awarded 5,901 diplomas, 341 certificates of honor, 25 medals for services to Grayovius, and 7,895 other award regalia."

Grayus looked respectfully at Shpik, who seemed to shrink in fear to half his height. Grayus paused, then continued.

"Here comes the most interesting part of your file, Shpik." Grayus squinted his eyes slyly as he looked at him before turning back to the document.

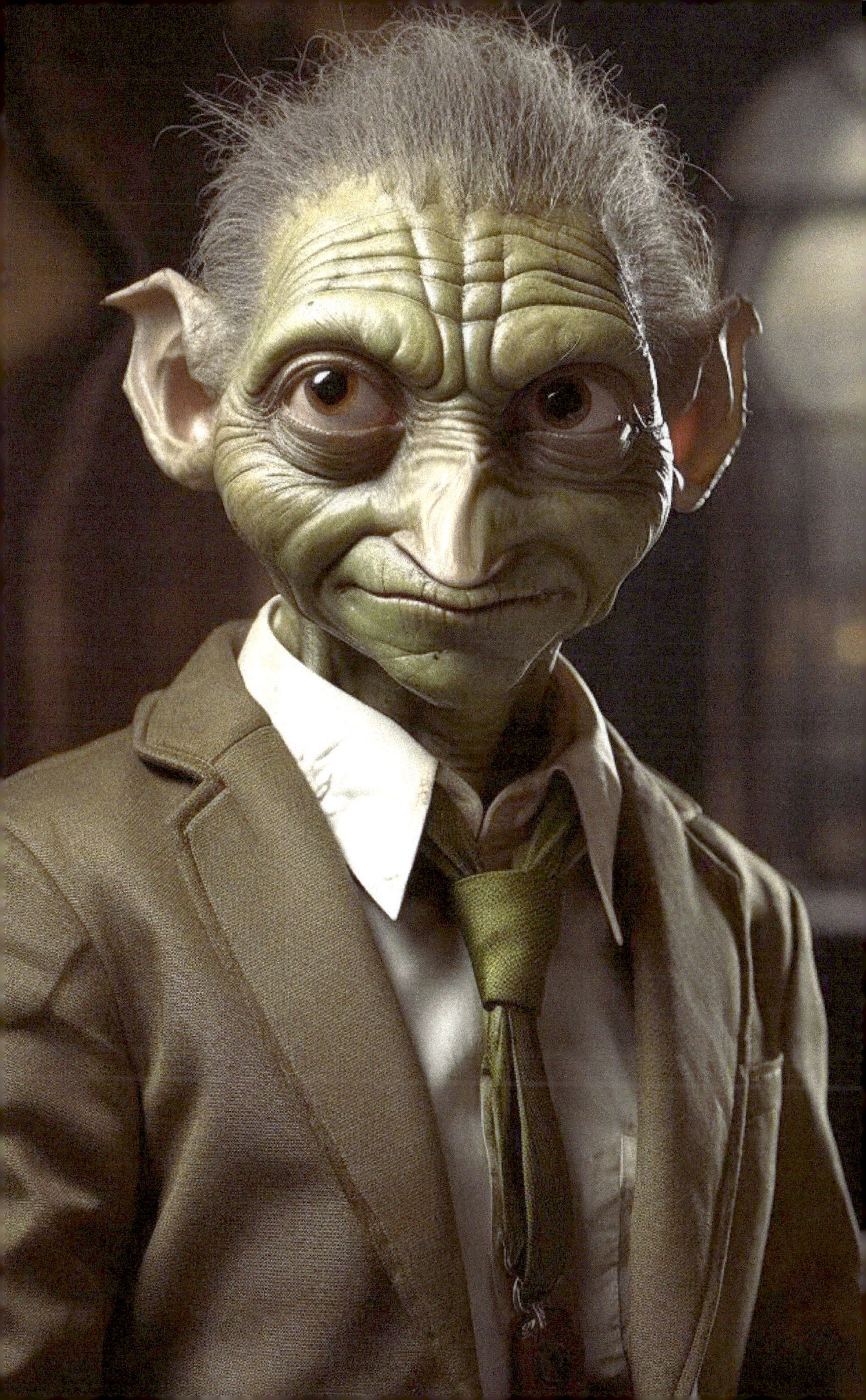

"My secret police have been following you for a long time, my unique friend. What do we have here? During your service, you took advantage of your official position and committed 15,528 illegal manipulations that created 65 coups d'état, 88 military conflicts, 97 tyrants, dictators, and other destroyers, and introduced 179 species of various diseases and other deadly viruses to the largest human-doll populations. As a result, your actions led to the destruction of an estimated 150 million human-dolls."

Grayus loudly slammed the folder; Shpik shuddered from surprise.

Grayus looked at him viciously and continued.

"All these things add up to nothing in comparison with your brazen and completely adventurist plan to carry out a coup here in Grayovius right under my nose."

He turned his eyes to the hump on his huge nose and smirked as if trying to lick the hump. Shpik could barely restrain a smirk of his own.

Grayus looked at him closely while reading out the verdict. Poor Shpik's heart felt as though it was fiercely stabbed and squeezed at the same time. Grayus paused for a bit and then laughed with all his voice, clutching his stomach out of pain from laughter.

"Ahh, if only you could see your face just now, Shpik," said Grayus through laughter and tears.

"Well, it doesn't fit a stitch with your talents for you to behave so defiantly."

"Will you execute me?" asked Shpik with sorrow.

Grayus looked at him with a cunning smile and slowly continued with a pinch of conspiratorial sarcasm.

"I have already executed you, as I have 2,358 other conspirators. Unlike them, you're still alive, my dear friend. Although, at the same time, you're officially dead. You're too valuable to me just to kill you. You will become part of my weapon, my power, my personal collection of omnipotence. Forget your name forever. Now, you're my servant, and your name is Chubata."

Grayus lit up at the crestfallen look on the newly minted servant's face.

"Please, do not thank me, buddy! I know this is a great honor for you. Now, let's talk about your most important task. I will have you destroy a group of four intrusive aliens who have invaded one of my farms." Grayus looked at him with a serious face, and Chubata perked up and even seemed to increase in height.

"As a reward for completion of this most important task, I will allow you to engage in whatever fascinates you the most in your free time—play tyrants, dictators, and whatever else you like. I don't care." After these words, Chubata rushed to bow down to Grayus' feet.

"I sweag on my ggatitude fog spaging my life to segve you with faith and tguth, my magnificent masteg."

With a gloating, satisfied smirk, Grayus gave Chubata's head a fatherly pat and imagined the coming reprisals against the aliens.

# Chapter 20

# The Cat Race

*In a perfect world, all the people would be like cats are at two o'clock in the afternoon.*

Gregory David Roberts, *Shantaram*

The cool night breeze blew pleasantly over Basil and Amandine's fluffy fur. They had gone out for some late-night running, adapting to the nocturnal modus operandi of their temporary cat bodies.

"You know, my dearest, I can't help but love these people. Let me tell you a true story that happened to one family," said Basil.

They teleported to a small town where it had just rained heavily. As he continued the story, it unfolded before them as if they were watching a movie.

"A two-month-old kitten sought refuge under a car to escape the rain. As the intimidating thud of large raindrops echoed on the hood, he crept deeper inside the vehicle, positioning himself near the hydro-amplifying belt. Unaware, a father and his daughter got into the car and started driving. Suddenly, the steering wheel jammed. They halted and stepped out to inspect the issue, when suddenly, a small red kitten emerged from beneath the left wheel of the car.

"His right front paw had been cut off, and they wanted to take him home, but the kitten quickly jumped into a fluffy bush by the road. They couldn't find him and thought he had probably died. They were very sad and shared the story with their family. Their family's ten-year-old boy heard the story and told his friends about it. Three days later, the children found the kitten alive and brought him to the daughter. She gave him water and food and took him to the vet, where he underwent successful surgery.

"The next day, she picked up her new friend from the hospital and bought everything he needed, including toys and a fluffy red bed in the shape of a tiger. The kitten chose the name Armani for himself; of all the names the girl tried to call him, he only responded to that one.

"The girl's parents became very attached to the kitten right away and were happy to welcome

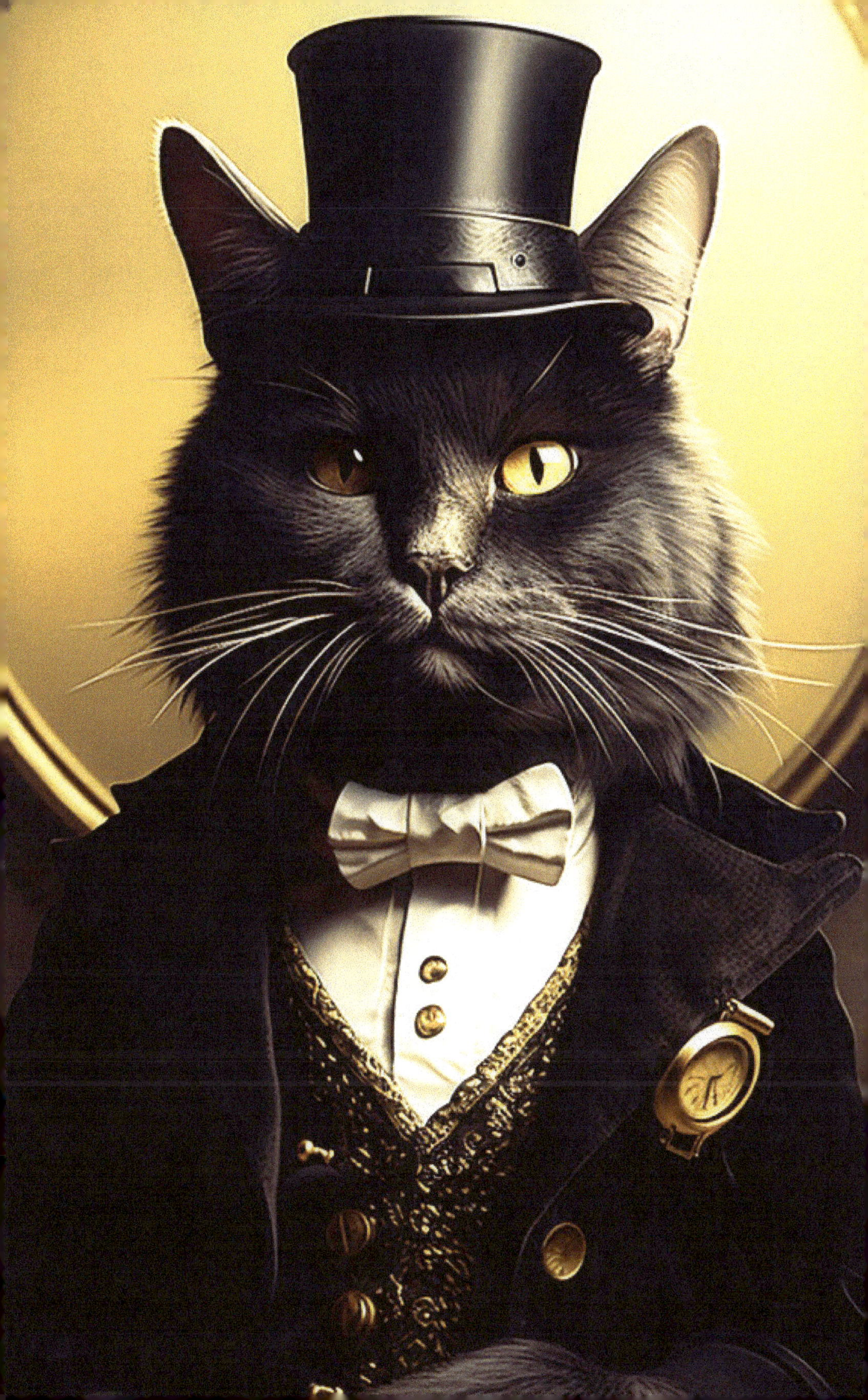

their new friend into their home. Now, he lives a good life and brings joy to the whole family with his brave, playful, and cheerful personality."

By the time he finished the story, they had teleported back to Grayville, where they continued running.

"The story is an amazing experience of one family!" Said Basil to his fluffy girlfriend.

"The Artist was right when he advised the chief agrobiologist to populate the planet Ambassador with animals suitable for domestication. These animals educate humans about compassion and all-forgiving love. Some people grasp and understand the concept, but most of them still have a lot to learn," said Amandine, her face showing a thoughtful expression.

After a moment, they teleported back into their temporary, mesmerizing animal bodies and continued running toward home on the beautiful and tranquil night, guided by the moonlight illuminating their path.

# Chapter 21

# The Secret Recipe

*The discovery of a good drink is more beneficial for mankind than any other discovery.*

Rafała Wiśniewskiego's Personal Journal

As soon as all members of the household had fallen asleep with sweet dreams, Baltz slowly left the bedroom and came into the living room. He took a flask of honey krupnik from its hiding spot, along with an old scroll and a well-worn directory of medicinal herbs, and quietly went to the veranda for some fresh night air.

He spun the top from the flask, looked around fearfully, and took a big sip. The honey krupnik spread a pleasant warmth throughout his body. After taking a sip, all his previous worries about the cats sighting that had been keeping him awake seemed to vanish into thin air. He smirked at himself for allowing those worries to brew in his head for such a long time and began to enjoy the quiet and beautiful surroundings of the veranda. Baltz peacefully looked at the clear, starry night sky and saw a shooting star. He made a wish and smiled at witnessing such a good omen.

He imagined climbing into the booth of his steam locomotive and knowledgeably examining the pressure gauge, which should not have been less than thirteen psi. In the coal car, junior assistant Karl filled the tray with coal, threw it into the furnace, and occasionally pumped water. Baltz closed the door of the boiler, pumped water to the desired mark, opened the siphon, pulled the reverser forward, and released the main brake. However, for the steam locomotive to depart, it was essential not to forget to release the "boy" or a small brake. If the "boy" were not released, the steam locomotive would shake furiously, but would not move.

He deeply inhaled to fill his full lungs with fresh air, then calmly exhaled and took another noble sip of his favorite drink. Slowly, his thoughts returned to the recent miracle he had witnessed alongside his partner. He blamed the whole incident on some ingredient of honey krupnik, but so far, he could not understand which one. From his pocket, he took out his grandfather's old secret recipe for this divine drink, written in Polish. Voraciously, he searched through it, looking for the cause of his troubles.

## Przepis na Miodowy Krupnik Rafała Wiśniewskiego (Wielkanoc, 1735 rok)

- 7 gram anyżu (7 grams anise)
- 10 gram kwiatów i liści piołunu (10 grams wormwood)
- 500 gram miodu (500 grams honey)
- 10 gram lasek wanilii (10 grams vanilla pods)
- 8 gram goździków (8 grams cloves)
- 10 gram cynamonu (10 grams cinnamon)
- 10 gram kolendry (10 grams coriander)
- 7 gram trawa żubrowa (7 grams bison grass)
- 20 gram jagody jałowca (20 grams juniper berries)
- 2 gramy gałki muszkatołowej (2 grams nutmeg)
- 6 gram kapsli kardamonu (6 grams cardamom pods)
- 950 ml alkoholu 55% (950 ml 55% alcohol)
- 650 ml alkoholu 50% (650 ml 50% alcohol)

Bądź zdrowy i bogaty! Na zdrowie! Rafał Wiśniewskie, 8 kwietnia, 1735 rok.

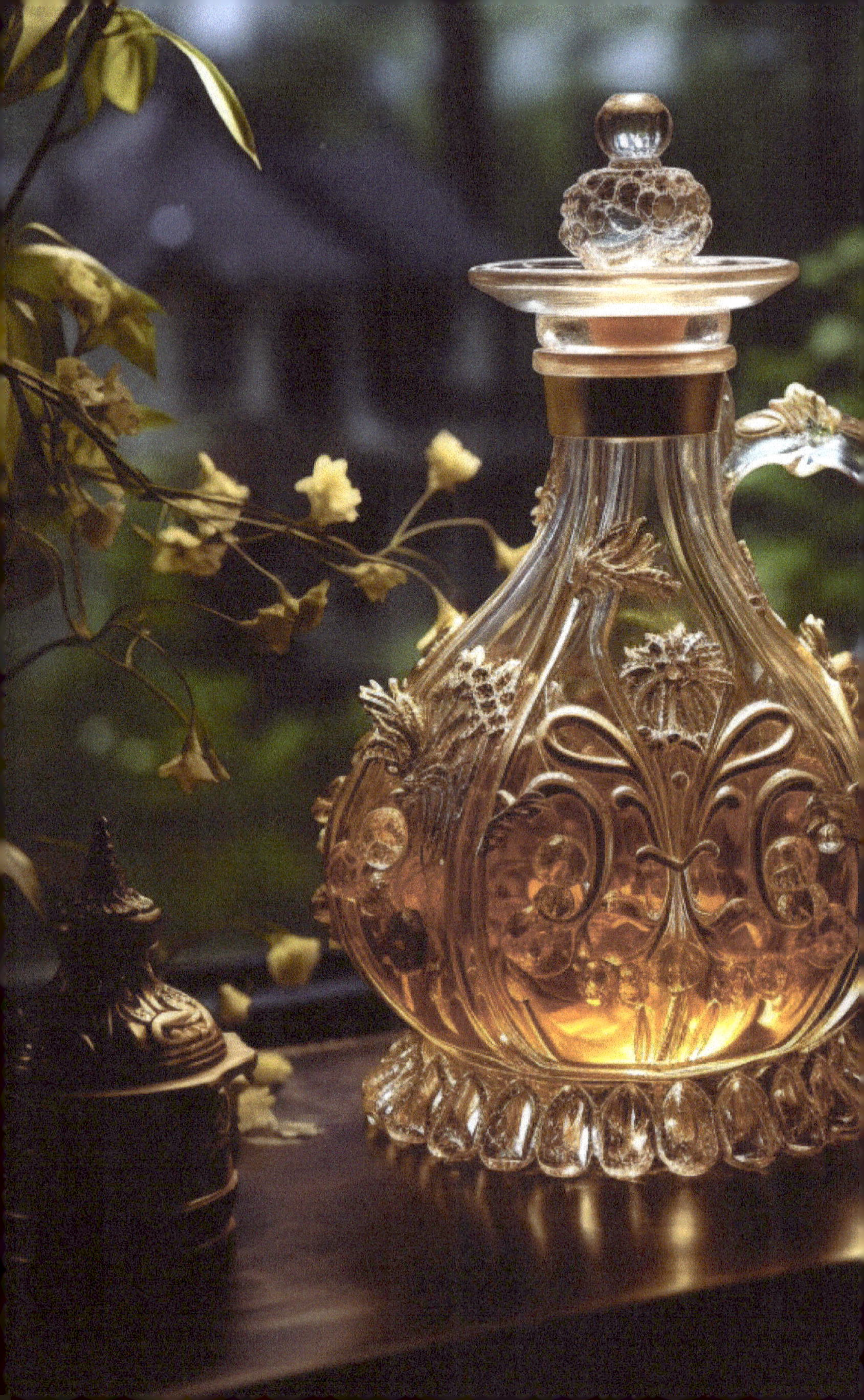

He opened the directory of medicinal herbs and scrupulously looked up each ingredient to find out which one could cause hallucinations. Wormwood was the only ingredient he found with noteworthy side effects, so he decided to exclude it from the next batch. With a sigh of relief, he looked around the neighborhood and saw a couple on a night run in the alley close to his house.

Baltz stayed still and quiet to avoid detection and find out who was running so late at night. When the couple approached his house, he could not believe his eyes. The two cats, which he thought he had imagined a couple of days ago, ran by on their hind paws, talking cheerfully. They waved happily as they passed Baltz's house and continued down the alley without slowing their pace.

Baltz's jaw fell to the floor. He dropped the flask, which hit the floor with a roar and prompted a scream from his wife.

"Baltz! You old fool! Again, you apply yourself to krupnik at night! You'll see. I'll show you the magic of the black eye!! Come back to bed immediately!"

He ran to the bedroom and, having gotten a leszcz[2] from his wife, went to bed in horror.

---

2   **"Leszcz"** is a Polish word that translates to "bream" in English, referring to a type of freshwater fish. Within the Polish context, the expression "to get a bream" means to receive a strong slap in the face.

# Chapter 22

# The MTech 5000

*Yes, yes, it was my idea to make available part of the virtual reality technology for our wards on the surface of the Earth.*

> Technical Director at Manipulation Technology, Inc., GBC News Interview

Chubata entered his new office, which now also doubled as his home. The door closed automatically behind him. Inside, he found everything necessary for a comfortable life. Gentle artificial sunlight fell on the floor through the window. The new place was at least ten times larger than his old apartment and featured a bar, kitchen, shower, jacuzzi, billiards room, home cinema, and even a small pool. A soft bed—huge, by his standards—sat in the corner, and nearby, there was a small table with a hologram screen for viewing work materials and Grayovius' most popular newspapers and magazines. A robot assistant worked in the kitchen, preparing breakfast. In another corner, Chubata saw something that made his jaw drop: a brand-new, fully operational, and highly technological machine for high-precision and ultra-high-speed manipulation. The MTech 5000.

The machine was equipped with an anatomical chair and a stepping surface under the feet, a virtual helmet, limb synchronization drives, four hyper-mobile monitors on liquid 10D crystals, a convertible manual control panel, a soundproofing dome, a subconscious control module, an intuitive analyzer, a synchronization and consciousness control module, a voice synchronizer-modulator, and, most importantly, a personality change module that could meet specified parameters (at the discretion of the operator!) with fully unlocked default persona settings. The core of this advanced technology was a 5,000-qubit quantum supercomputer, with processing power more than ten times greater than that of all existing shmyg computers combined. This technological wonder was very pleasing to Chubata, to say the least.

The innovation was entirely secret and existed as a single copy, intended for special covert operations according to Grayus' design. The new machine made it possible to get inside any human-doll of any race whenever and wherever in the world, which meant the machine made it possible for shmygs to move in time and space. However, the device only allowed manipulations in the present; the most decorated shmyg scientists were working on achieving manipulations in the past and the future.

Chubata watched the long instruction video and was overjoyed and excited to get in there and get his hands dirty. He dropped into the chair and his eyes rolled in ecstasy. It felt as though power over the entire world permeated every cell of his body. As he closed his eyes and completely sank into the chair, his legs were lifted off the floor, and the chair took the shape of his body, wrapping him in a comfortable cocoon. The helmet descended onto his head, and consciousness synchronization began. It ended so swiftly that he did not even comprehend its conclusion, unlike his past job, where he often fell asleep waiting for synchronization to complete. His thoughts appeared on the screen.

"The choice is extraordinary personalities." His consciousness indicated a number. "184,765."

The next thought occurred.

"Current selection is a random object."

Within his consciousness, he heard the artificial intelligence's pleasant voice, specifically selected for him based on the primary analysis of his brain that had happened during synchronization.

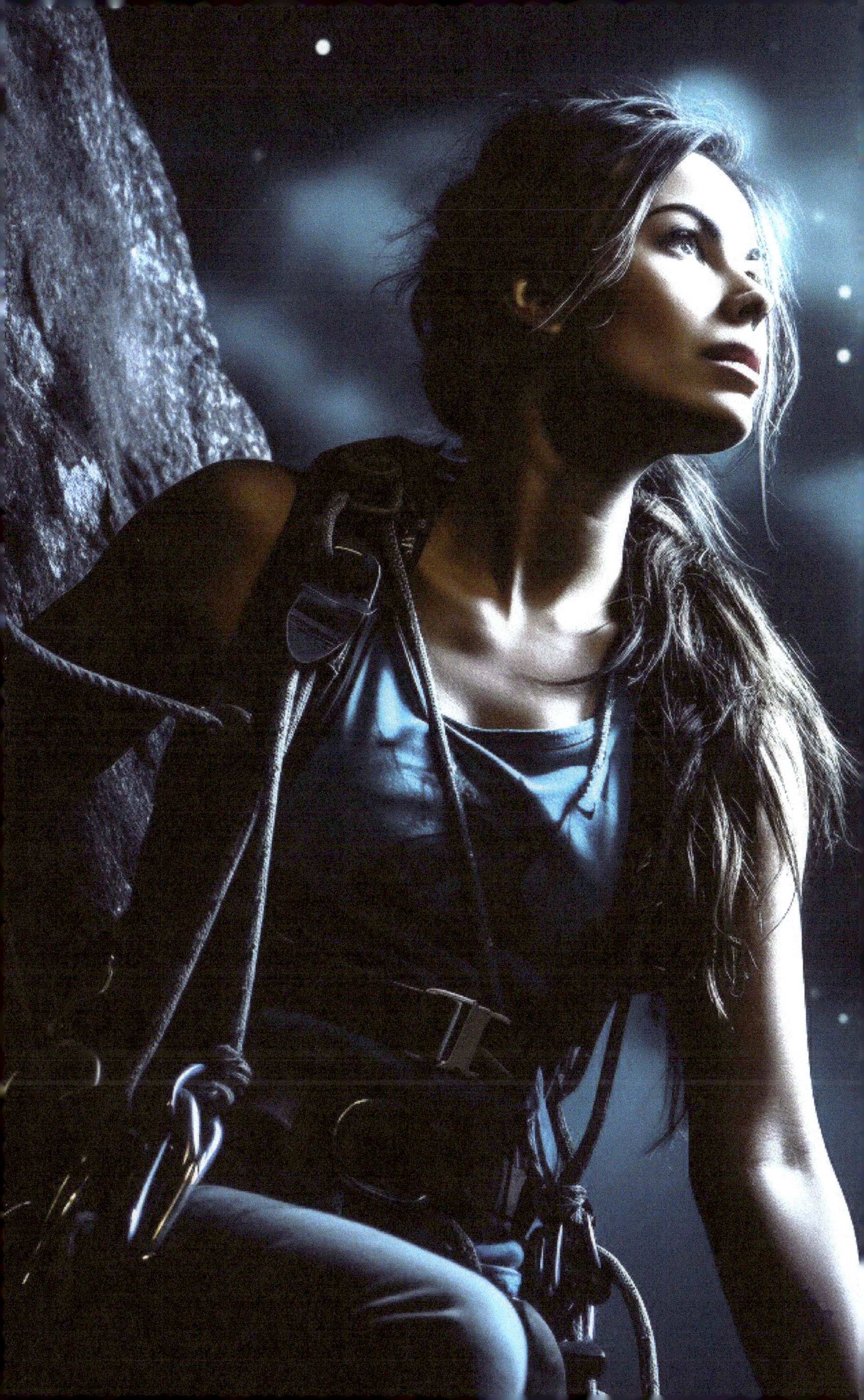

"The object number is 4,768. It was chosen absolutely and utterly by chance, based on the Theory of Chaos and Incredible Coincidences. Time: 22:00 p.m. Month: September. Day: 20th. Year: 1994. Would you like me to start synchronizing?"

"Yes, please."

Chubata only had time for a brief moment of thought before he found himself in the body of a woman. At this point, he could only watch and listen.

"Are you holding me, Matt?" The young woman asked calmly, standing at the base of the mountain.

"Let's check the equipment again. The rope serves us well. Everything is good with your belay device. The knot is shaped in a figure eight and tied correctly."

She put two fingers to the knot and counted.

"Two, two, and two. Yeah, haha. It's okay! Safety equipment sits tight, fastened correctly at the waist and on the hips."

The young woman looked up at the stars, then smiled at her partner and lowered her fingers into her chalk bag. She shook her hands and began to climb up amidst a symphony of sounds from quick-draws, nuts, hexes, and a couple of iron flasks of water hooked to the harness belt.

"Good luck and enjoy the Nose! I heard upstairs there's a great bar where they serve the best margaritas in Yosemite! All that remains is to get up there, girl!" Matt joked encouragingly.

She climbed without stopping, thinking about nothing but her movements on the rock.

"Real freedom!" She thought to herself.

Her thoughts poured into her head slowly and calmly.

"All of it is familiar and even native to me. Each movement, each pull of the hand and foot, should be as effective as possible so as not to waste strength and to get to the top of the cliff at the scheduled time. Granite stone becomes slippery with time. I need to save the chalk powder and use it only if necessary. Your body knows everything, so trust it and listen to your instincts. Let this free flow inside! Just go with it all the way up to the top!"

She was relaxed but climbed up with concentration, not giving in to her fear or negative emotions.

"I feel great! Such a beautiful and bright full moon lights up my way on the rock. I feel as if I am one with the mountain. It's like I'm flying over the rock with zero gravity."

She looked like a spider, clinging with her legs and hands to the narrow protrusions of a flat rock. Night climbing was sometimes insidious, shading false support spots for hands and legs, but it was also an extraordinary and fascinating experience.

Time and distance flew out of the woman's head; only her movements on the mountain were important. All her thoughts switched to a narrow focus. She admired the bird's eye view now and then.

She subconsciously arrived at a state of meditation and enjoyed every movement.

She had trained well to achieve the stamina required to spend such a long time on a climb. She had previously spent a long time on other mountains and easily conquered peaks around the world. The night was calm and quiet, with the exception of bats and night bugs that sometimes flew by her. The two brave people were climbing up the rock that night, completely unaware that they were making history.

The dawn came slowly, gradually illuminating El Capitan's granite walls.

"The dawn begins to tickle the peaks, and we've spent approximately eight hours on the rock. More than a third of the path has been traveled, about 1,100 feet. Good speed. View from above, simply picturesque!"

The thoughts calmly left her, and she took a complex step, crossing her feet and pulling up with her hands, holding on to a narrow ledge with just her fingertips.

The sun had risen, illuminating Yosemite Valley and the huge granite monolith of El Capitan. The partners continued their journey, and the brave woman led the climbing path, laying the rope with the gear as if weaving a web. She felt severe fatigue, and her body ached in different places from a great load, but she did not succumb to this feeling. Instead, she switched her thoughts to a prideful sense of endurance and appreciation for the path she had made. She continued to climb up the rock with sincere curiosity for new adventures.

By the time she reached 2,000 feet, it seemed to the woman that she was communicating with the rock, as if the rock prompted her to choose the right support spots for her hands and feet. Not paying attention to her fatigue, she enjoyed the feeling of freedom and self-control.

"Another lead. The iron nut goes into this crack, and I pull on it—it sits tightly in the crack of the mountain. I pass the rope through the quickdraw. A bit closer to the target; the main thing is to keep moving forward! The left hand and right foot are in good support spots. Pulling with the left hand against the rock, I step over with the left foot, push slightly, and grab onto the next ledge with the right hand. Great! Now, holding on with my hands and the left foot, I move my right leg up. The view is indescribable!"

The sky began to darken, and the shimmering stars called out to the silver girlfriend, the full moon. She had a few hours left to meet her goal. Only 300 feet remained. All her movements were premeditated and vaguely familiar. The fearless young woman gracefully continued as if she were a ballerina, completing her pirouettes one after another. Her partner, with admiration, followed her path. One smooth movement up replaced another smooth movement up, hand after hand, foot after foot.

"Every movement is another small victory in itself! I can do so much more. Just keep going! I'm still at the very beginning, and how much more remains to be done."

The woman made the last leap, leaning over the support spot with the right side of her body at the top of the granite wall. Slowly pulling herself up, she grasped a small ledge on the top of the peak with her left hand. Clinging to the rocks at the top, she pulled her body up and over the cliff.

"Yes, Leann!! You made it—the first free ascent of the Nose on El Capitan in less than twenty-four hours! Thank you!"

The woman stood strong and tall while smiling at the amazing view in front of her.

# Chapter 23

# The Theory of Chaos & Incredible Coincidences

*The wave of a butterfly wing at one end of the globe could cause a hurricane at another end of the globe.*

Albrecht Schmychtis,
*The Theory of Chaos and Incredible Coincidences*

About 50,000 years ago, the famous shmyg scientist Albrecht Schmychtis refuted most of the laws of physics, thermodynamics, and materialism, proving that any object in the universe, including intangible ones, has at least one unstable oscillatory point. By correctly affecting this point, it is possible to bring the object into a state of chaos with unpredictable consequences. In the experiment, he calculated this unstable point on the basis of the Theory of Chaos and Incredible Coincidences: "An event that cannot happen under any circumstances will not occur if even one necessary condition for its occurrence is absent in another quantum parallelism."

The experimental laboratory was, of course, Earth. The respected scientist took an ordinary walnut-sized stone, placed it in a gravitational capsule, and affected one certain electron of one of the hydrogen atoms inside the stone with a short-term quantum impulse. At this moment, a fifty-meter meteorite, calmly drifting through the expanses of the universe and not posing any danger to Earth, suddenly changed its trajectory and, at a speed of more than 60,000 kilometers per hour, began heading directly to the planet's surface. This powerful explosion left a crater 1,200 meters across and more than 1,080 meters deep. At that time, no one considered the loss of the wild tribes of human-dolls; the meteorite did not cause any harm to the shmygs located deep underground. The crater exists to this day in Arizona, and attracts many tourists because of its size.

At the time, the scientist received universal recognition, and the experiment gave impetus to the development of a completely new field in science: the manipulation of consciousness. After all, a person could be affected just like the meteorite, and plunged into a state of controlled chaos.

The first prototypes of consciousness control were created. Through the shmygs' influence, humans' lives gradually changed for the better. They learned to talk, make fire, and build homes. They invented wheels, iron axes, and spears. They sewed clothes and engaged in agriculture and animal domestication. Then, the first scientists, philosophers, and doctors appeared. Soon thereafter, they united in larger social groups and formed larger settlements and communities. In the end, they united in one single civilization, spoke the same language, and had one noble goal: universal well-being.

Humans were grown like plants in a garden raised by an attentive and caring gardener, and gradually provided with more knowledge. The shmygs took good care of the humans for a long time.

However, sooner or later, all good things must come to an end. Disagreements about the ways of new civilization development grew among shmygs. Some of them were opposed to providing humans with so much knowledge and technology, while others talked about uniting with humans.

Consequently, Earth was partitioned among the highest-caste clans of shmygs, each ruling their domain with the power to forge their destiny. In this realm of enchantment, clans held the reigns to sculpt their own path, embarking on unique journeys of growth and ingenuity. This autonomy paved the way for the shmygs, mystical beings who cultivated dollcoins from the fabric of human dreams, to bestow upon humanity the arcane knowledge of cryptocurrency in later stages of their development.

This division birthed nations, each with its distinct languages and cultures, spreading across the globe. When conflicts brewed within the underground realms of shmyg clans, they were mirrored above in turmoil on the surface. Earth became a battleground for relentless wars, fueled by disputes and discord. Ambitions for dominance, control, and insatiable greed infected societies. As civilizations halted their progress, consumed by the strife, they plunged into the arms race of devising ever more devastating weapons, including those of biological nature, forsaking development for destruction.

All of this would have led to the near destruction of this new world, had it not been for one particular incident that occurred just in time at another end of the universe on a planet similar to Earth... The iridescent blue butterfly fluttered its beautiful wings...

# Chapter 24

# Pentoball

*In 5,000 years of my career as an anchorman, I have never seen anyone survive the Ceremony of Forgiveness.*

Smih Shmurk, GBC News

Spectators filled the millennial stadium, Santa Del Penta. Motley shmygs from all kinds of castes, communities, and clans of Grayovius sat in their places, waiting for the start of the ceremony. The atmosphere of the holiday was in the air, and the crowd buzzed in anticipation of the annual celebration. A transparent electromagnetic dome, about thirty meters across, sat in the center of the stadium.

Inside the dome, on a tungsten-iridium plate about three meters high, there were 200 shackled shmygs of different heights, from less than a half-meter tall to meter-high giants.

In the center of the dome, in a powerful electromagnetic field, about two meters above the ground, hung a clot of dream quasi-matter of the pento category. It vibrated with an enormous kinetic energy, looking for a weak point in its restraining field.

AI-powered camera drones flew everywhere, broadcasting every corner of this long-awaited holiday throughout Grayovius. Hundreds of millions of viewers gathered at home to watch the ceremony on hologram screens, eagerly awaiting its start.

The anthem of Grayovius played next to the dome. Soon after that, the show's host, Smih Shmurk, appeared on a flying platform, brightly illuminated by many spotlights.

"Greetings to you, my dear viewers, from the incredible, mind-blowing, delightful, teeth-breaking, crushing, merciless, and most amazing..." the presenter made a significant pause and then continued in a loud voice, "annual Ceremony of Fo-o-orrrgi-i-ivne-e-e-ss!!!"

Cheers and applause drowned the stadium. The audience jumped up from their seats and continued to shout words of admiration. The presenter circled the dome, fueled by the spectators' energy, then stopped right above the dome and enthusiastically continued his theatrical speech.

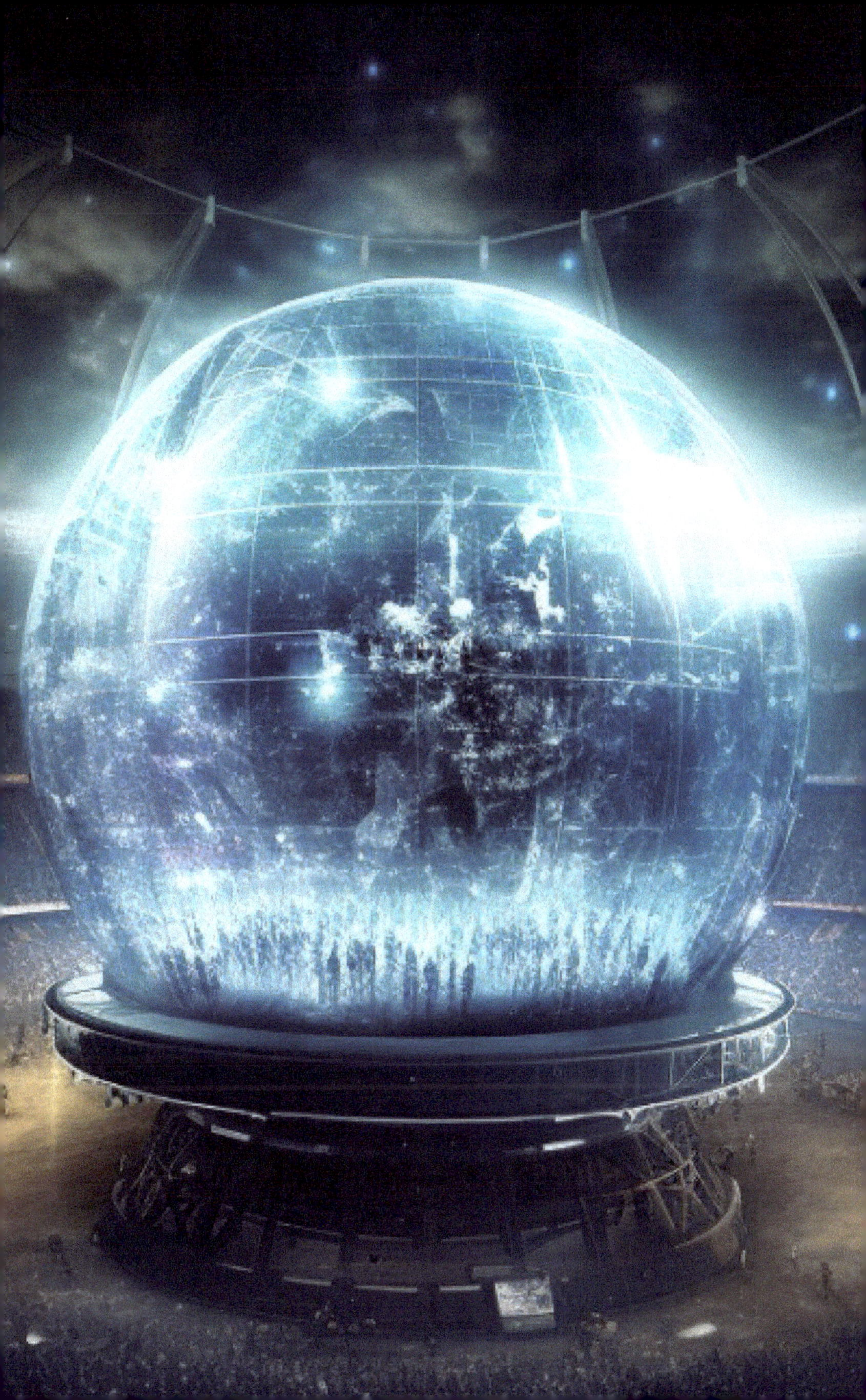

"In this piece of dream qusi-matter," he pointed down toward the pento, "there is enough kinetic energy to destroy half of this stadium and its audience."

An alarmed buzz swept through the stadium.

"However, our engineers were able to curb this unbroken horse and, believe me, it will never get out of this dome."

The crowd made a sound of total relief.

"I would like to remind you that over twenty thousand years ago, the Most Honorable Shmyg Council of the Ancients of Grayovius offered even the most notorious criminals a chance to clear their names and become full-fledged citizens of Grayovius again, having passed the Ceremony of Forgiveness. This great honor today falls to the 200 criminals sentenced to death."

He paused for a moment, then pointed toward the three judges sitting in a special lodge and continued.

"Please greet our esteemed judges!"

A hum of greeting swept through the stadium.

"Before each of them, there is a green button that they will press, if they decide to pardon the unfortunates. Only if all three press this button will the unbridled dream quasi-matter be deactivated and the surviving criminals pardoned."

The host flew around the dome and stopped near one of the huge shmygs inside the dome, obscured by a shadow. The camera displayed the shmyg's silhouette, and the host continued in a conspiratorial voice.

"Among the criminals today, there is one unique personality. He is someone whom each of you may know. He is the one who turned away from the law-abiding shmygs. The one who conceived the worst crime! Someone who was amazed by the idea of obscurantism of equality and brotherhood!"

He paused, and the whole stadium froze in anticipation. The presenter sharply flew off to the side, and the spotlight illuminated the shmyg.

"Tiibeeriyiuus!!!" Thousands of shmygs screamed with excited delight. Many of them cried with happiness.

"Greet your unmatched champion because he has a chance to be pardoned, like all these criminals today."

Tiberius stood straight and was extremely focused, like an athlete before a game. The presenter retreated to a spectating area. With three short beeps, the shackles fell, and the dream quasi-matter broke out of the restraining field and began to dismember the poor shmygs like lightning. From the outside, everything looked like a huge meat grinder; the hands, legs, and heads of the unfortunate shmygs scattered in different directions.

Tiberius made a sharp swerve to the side when his shackles came off, avoiding the first blow. Out of the corner of his eye, he saw a barely noticeable portal.

He dodged the second blow and, without losing speed, glided along the surface of the tungsten-iridium plate and rolled into the portal, which immediately slammed behind him. But the viewers could only see the bloody mess of the other criminals.

The ceremony lasted no longer than five seconds before the judges simultaneously pressed the green buttons. After several inert blows, the deactivated dream quasi-matter slowed and then completely stopped.

The presenter dryly delivered the final speech.

"The ceremony was successfully completed. Today, 200 criminals were denied clemency."

# Chapter 25

# The Psychotherapist

*Fritz Pörlez is the only shmyg scientist who has recreated the exact integrity of his personality in the world of humans without resorting to manipulation!*

A quote from the documentary,
*The Greatest Shmygs of Grayovius*

Every Wednesday for the last hundred years, Grayus had attended sessions with the renowned psychotherapist, the honored academician of the Medical Academy of Science of Grayovius, professor of the faculty of psycho-correction, Dr. Fritz Pörlez. Dr. Pörlez was the only shmyg in the universe who Grayus respected—and the only one he feared to his core.

He sat modestly on a chair in the doctor's reception room, humbly awaiting his turn without a shred of dissatisfaction. Many high-ranking shmygs of different stripes waited in line alongside him: the Supreme Judge, the Chief Prosecutor, a famous billionaire, and even a member of the Shmyg Council of the Ancients. All knew each other perfectly well. However, at the doctor's office, there was an unspoken rule: please observe the world in silence. None of them wanted to upset the doctor or bring trouble to themselves. Therefore, all patients sat silently, not acknowledging anyone around.

After about half an hour, they heard the cheerful voice of the doctor's assistant from the wall speaker.

"Patient number 348, Dr. Pörlez is ready for you!"

Grayus quickly rose from his chair and approached the entrance. The door had a sign on it with the inscription: A crazy shmyg said, "I am Abraham Lincoln." A neurotic shmyg said, "I would like to be like Abraham Lincoln." A healthy shmyg said, "I am being myself, and you are being yourself."

Grayus stopped in front of the door for a moment, gathering his thoughts. His legs were shaking, and anxiety overtook his mind. Finally, he collected himself and entered the office. The doctor sat on a couch behind a small coffee table, smiling and at ease. He nodded his head in greeting to Grayus and invited him to sit down next to him. Grayus proceeded fearfully and sat down. He looked at his feet, nervously drumming his fingers like a guilty schoolboy in the headmaster's office.

"Where are you?" asked the doctor, smiling.

Grayus looked around incredulously and uttered, "At your office during our session."

"What are you doing now?" the doctor continued, still smiling.

"I am sitting on a couch and answering your questions," answered Grayus. He never knew what the doctor would throw at him.

The doctor jumped sharply from the couch and, with all his might, slapped Grayus hard on his face. Slightly in pain, Grayus scratched the back of his head and cringed a little.

"How do you feel now?" The doctor asked with a paternal smile as if nothing had happened.

"I feel pain and resentment," said Grayus, barely holding back his tears.

The doctor got up and stroked Grayus on the head. "Well, now, how do you feel?"

"I feel confusion, uncertainty, and a little more pain," Grayus answered, his voice tinged with a mix of vulnerability and resilience.

"Now, let's hold our hands and say our message together," said Dr. Pörlez. They held their hands up and began to speak at the same time, looking at each other.

"I do my job, and you do your job. I'm not in this world to meet your expectations, and you are not

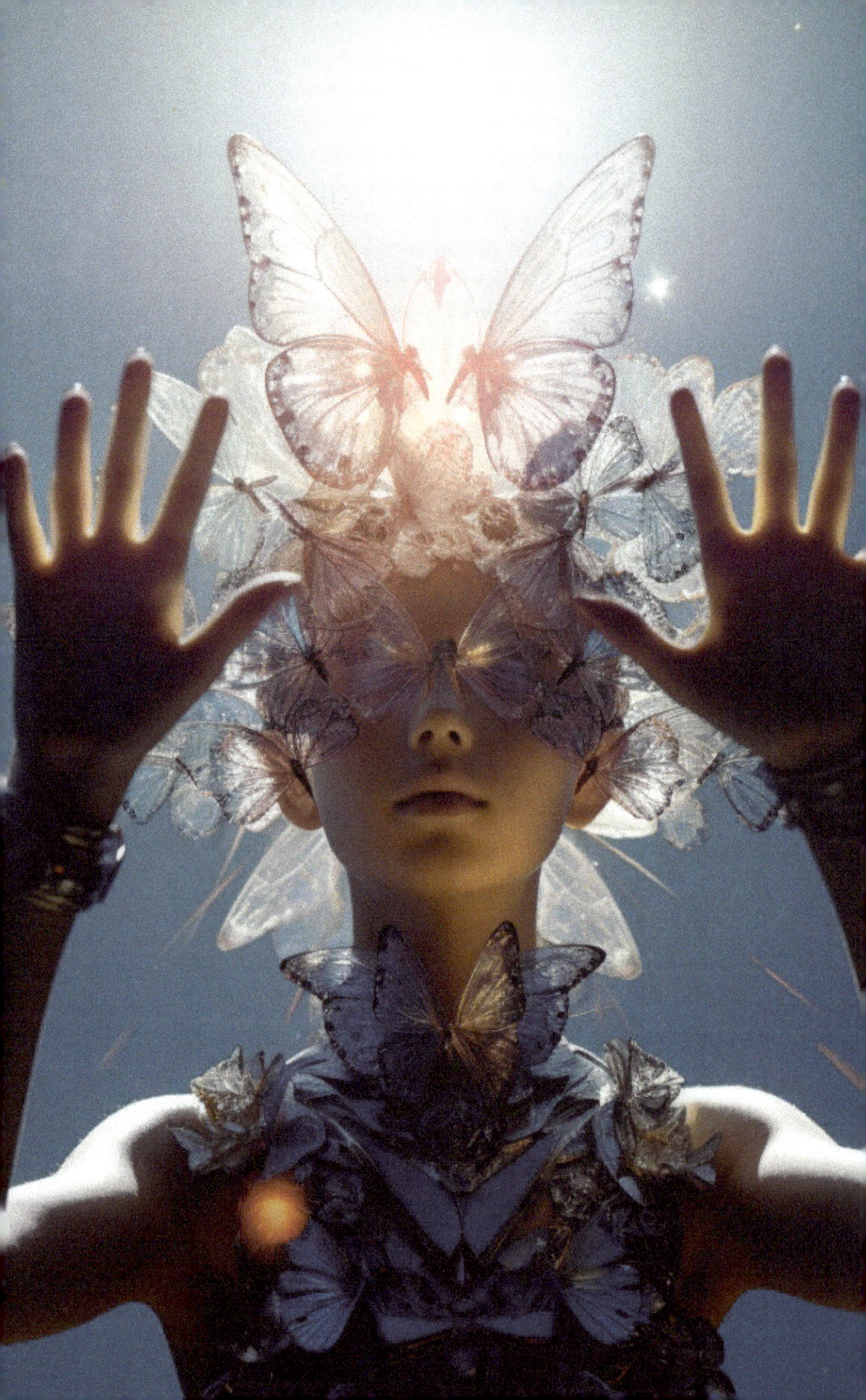

in this world to meet mine. You are being yourself, and I am being myself. If we happen to find each other, that's fine; if not, you can't help it."

As soon as they finished, the doctor sat more comfortably in his chair, evaluating Grayus. After a moment, he spoke with emphasis.

"I always repeat to my patients that our id is priceless and its boundaries are sacred. This world is constantly trying to move these boundaries, aggressively attacking our individuality. You should not expect the world to treat you fairly just because you are good. That's like expecting a lion not to attack you because you're a vegetarian. Under the pressure of external influence, our id gets consumed and hides in the subconscious. Therefore, our individuality is replaced by a certain social sub-personality that is most convenient for the society in which we exist. That is why I strongly oppose the idea that society should completely destroy individuality. In the end, our id cannot stand it. It gets hidden in the subconscious and begins to attack this sub-personality in which we comfortably exist within society. As a result, we get a lot of neuroses, phobias, apathy, anxiety, and all kinds of other mental illnesses."

The doctor slowly rose from his chair and looked at Grayus with intensity. Grayus realized something bad was about to happen. The doctor picked up the chair and approached him steadily, looking like a maniac. Grayus slowly rose from the couch and backed toward the door without taking his eyes off the doctor. Suddenly, the doctor swung to hit Grayus with the chair and chased him down, screaming his throat out.

"Screw your sub-personality!!! Free your id!!!"

Grayus fled the office, stunned. Breathing hard, he closed the door behind him and leaned his back against it. Having caught sympathetic looks from other patients, he swiftly headed for the exit with confidence.

# Chapter 26

# Gestalt

*Human-dolls exhibit a strong tendency to use their brains only when faced with entirely new situations. They dislike applying their minds to modifying traditional procedures.*

Dr. Fritz Pörlez

The door to Chubata's office opened, and Grayus confidently walked inside like it was his own house. His servant, as always, worked hard; even now, he was inside the capsule chair. Grayus pressed the red emergency ejection button on the manipulation unit.

The capsule vibrated and made strange sounds as if it were choked with something foreign. After a split second, it spat Chubata out on the floor like chewed gum. He collapsed onto the floor with a roar of pain and frantically looked around.

When he saw Grayus standing before him, he jumped onto his feet, stretching tall like a metal pole. He stared at Grayus with a devoted look. Grayus gladly noted that the psycho-correction of his servant was going well. Now, he not only posed no threat but was also very loyal. He gave Chubata's head a paternal pat, and Chubata's eyes rolled up in joy. Like a dog anticipating affection, he moved his head toward Grayus' palm, eagerly awaiting more pats.

"What was my loyal servant doing today?" asked Grayus, smiling kindly.

"My fascination with a specific field of study in neurochemical manipulation, namely the neuroscience of attraction in human-dolls, has been long-standing. This interest has persisted from a time when I lacked the substantial resources necessary to conduct thorough scientific research.

"To our knowledge, it is impossible to remotely control human-dolls during a potent chemical response elicited by another's voice, scent, the dynamic essence of their gestures, and their visual allure. The human-dolls describe this phase as 'love.'

"Previously, to safeguard the remote manipulation controls used with human-dolls, we took painstaking measures to prevent any chemical bonding between them. Nevertheless, should an intense chemical interaction between human-dolls not be halted, it would necessitate the physical deployment of an elite emergency response team to overhaul and replace the manipulation and absorption mechanisms within both dolls.

"The science of neurochemical manipulation of human-dolls, particularly this facet, has captivated my interest due to my desire to challenge and potentially disprove this scientific assertion using a range of empirical techniques. Therefore, when I encountered a case of strong chemical bonding inside a human-doll, I dedicated my time to calibrating the doll. I named this the 'Doll in Love' module. I refined its optimization, identified entry points, performed multi-tiered scans of neural networks and psychological connections, synchronized consciousness, and conducted related scientific experiments." Chubata gave his report quickly and confidently, like an experienced army servant.

Grayus was very pleased. Psycho-correction had not only turned Chubata into a truly faithful servant but had also rectified the nasty speech disorder that annoyed Grayus so much.

"Well, well, my kind Chubata, please set out the details." Grayus deliberately addressed him with respectful kindness to reinforce the hidden parameters of psycho-correction, which he personally selected for him.

"For my study, I meticulously chose a human-doll entwined in a strong affectionate bond with his female companion. She, a lifelong vegan, had subtly guided him toward embracing a plant-based regimen. Residing in San Diego, he amassed a fortune of millions, presenting a psyche unmarred by disorders or psychological afflictions. His was a delta-tier personality—remarkably resilient to external persuasion, shifts in awareness, or psychological maneuvering."

The master listened to him with interest. Chubata interrupted his report for a moment and walked toward his bed. Then, he moved the small table with the hologram screen and placed it in front of Grayus. Chubata pressed a button on the remote to display a presentation on the screen.

"Please continue, my gracious friend." Grayus got comfortable in a chair, and Chubata continued.

Chubata's endeavors were devoted to an exhaustive analysis of the cerebral neural networks and synaptic interplays, seeking any latent susceptibilities. In due course, Chubata unearthed a pair of psychological enigmas. The initial paradox laid in the subject's indelible sensory imprint of barbecued pork—the first he had ever savored—at six years old during a family vacation. This stood in stark contrast to the current vegan ethos. The second anomaly laid in the hierarchy of the emotional allegiances. Conventionally, the intensity of familial and romantic chemical bonds followed a parallel path. However, in the subject's case, the departure of his much older and dearly beloved brother from the family after his very first family camping trip disproportionately strengthened his familial bonds. This incident with his brother leaving overshadowed the romantic affection he held for his female companion.

During those early, blissful years, with his family united and joyful, the subject savored the delights of the lively first family camping trip. The grandeur of nature had enveloped them as they convened in a scenic canyon abuzz with festive cheer. The occasion had forged an indelible link in his mind, intertwining the savor of flavors of barbecued pork with joyful, familial bonds. The flavors danced in his memory, a rich tapestry of spices, each contributing its unique note to the euphoric symphony of the flavors that marked a joyous day.

The subject could remember how the red pepper brought a lively kick, igniting a spark of excitement with every bite. The coriander added a refreshing hint of citrus that lightened the heart, while the cumin added a layer of warmth, bringing a comforting, spicy aroma that hugged the senses.

Each bite was a cascade of sensations, with garlic adding depth and robustness to the meat, enveloping it with a full-bodied aroma. The onions played a dual role, tenderizing the meat to succulent perfection while gracing it with a slight taste of sweetness that hinted at the joyous moments.

The barberry was the secret star, imparting a subtle tang that titillated the taste buds, its sour

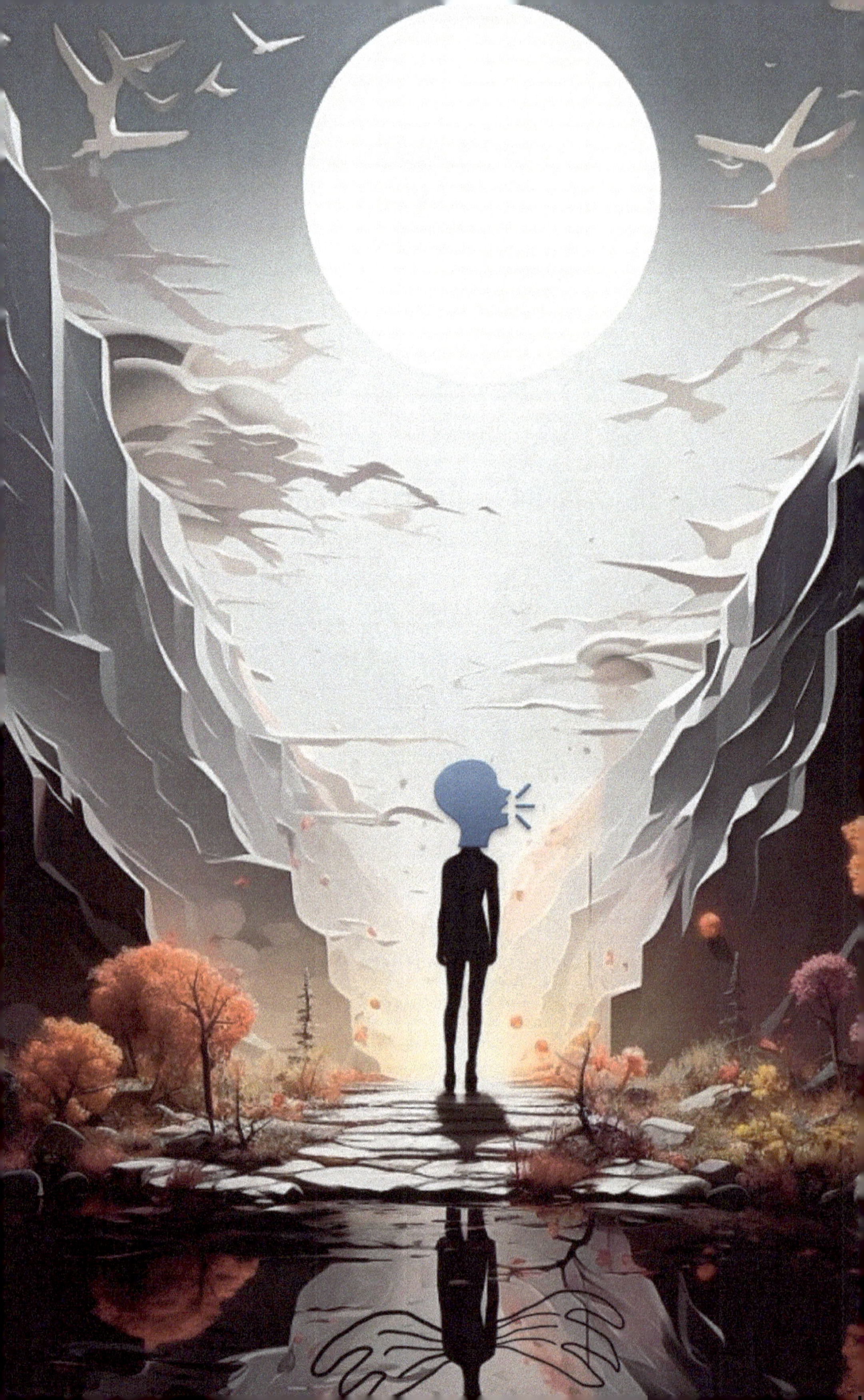

notes dancing joyfully amidst the medley of flavors. Every nuance of the marjoram and thyme echoed in the background, offering their herbal embrace to the composition and giving it a distinctive, aromatic signature that spoke of family, joy, and home. Crowning the medley of spices was the bay leaf, a gentle whisper in the symphony of flavors, bringing an exclusive aroma that tied all the elements together, knitting a tapestry of taste that was as unique as it was comforting.

"Merely discussing the subject of barbecue sets my salivary glands into overdrive. I must concede that this human-doll lineage possesses an exceptional culinary prowess when it comes to the art of barbecuing." Chubata wiped the saliva from his lips with a satisfied grin.

As the subject reminisced, every spice told a story, a memory etched in the canvas of his childhood, a testament to the joy and unity that the family celebration bestowed upon him. It was a flavor profile that was not just a meal but a vivid painting of happiness and familial love stuck in his heart, vivid and lingering, a joy forever associated with the warm embrace of family.

Further, to form a holistic picture, in accordance with the provisions of Dr. Fritz Pörlez's Gestalt psychology, Chubata only needed to provide the subject with an insight. It took Chubata three days.

As an outdoor enthusiast, the subject embarked on a rock-climbing adventure in California's Yosemite National Park. Grayus's humble servant brilliantly utilized the susceptibility of five easily manipulated, impressionable, and quite inebriated beta personalities to mastermind a meeting with the subject. Near the campsite where the subject and his friends were staying, the five beta personalities began to prepare a pork barbecue using the distinctive recipe that the subject knew all too well.

When he smelled the familiar aromas from the barbecue, it evoked his cherished childhood memories and he felt compelled to walk over and introduce himself to the group. Chubata captured the heartwarming scene of the subject engaging in a relaxed conversation with his newfound friends. This rapport echoed the ease and joy reminiscent of the time spent enjoying the special barbecue with his family outdoors. Chubata then fused this vivid dual imagery in the subject's mind with the previously identified first psychological anomaly and bingo! A moment of profound insight dawned upon the subject, illuminating his consciousness and bringing his objective into sharp focus. The subject was struck by an irresistible urge to taste a piece of meat from the barbecue. He took a piece of barbecued pork and put it into his watering mouth.

"At that juncture, the scenario was predominantly a question of technological orchestration. Historically, the subject reveled in climbing alongside close companions and his significant other, enjoying the camaraderie. Yet, the tapestry of his experiences underwent a stark transformation in the subsequent month," Chubata said proudly as he continued reporting the details of his research.

An overwhelming compulsion for a diverse array of meats engulfed the subject. His social existence flourished; weekends metamorphosed into festive congregations centered around ceremonial barbecue feasts, magnetizing an increasingly broad spectrum of acquaintances.

Strategically, Chubata utilized the second psychological anomaly to catalyze an epiphany within the subject—that this burgeoning cohort of barbecue aficionados was, in essence, an extension of his familial network. The realization deepened the subject's emotional investment in this new communal bond, concurrently attenuating the prominence of his romantic entanglement with his female companion.

Their periods of time alone significantly decreased as the subject's preference shifted toward hosting barbecue gatherings rather than partaking in al fresco ascents and rock-climbing trips with her. The frequency and intensity of their discord escalated with each passing day.

As their emotional connection diminished, it facilitated the embedding of more potent manipulative programming within both dolls. Chubata's interference further altered their lifestyle, igniting a robust libido and amplifying the subject's carnal urges. His gaze began to wander, drawn to the allure of other female dolls, making him more flirtatious. Subsequently, Chubata programmed the subject's female companion to experience heightened disappointment and resentment toward the subject.

"I masterminded for the subject to host an avant-garde barbecue soirée, whimsically dubbed *'Carnivale of Carnivore Couture,'* wherein the male attendees were to attire themselves as an array of charcuterie and the female guests as a medley of artisanal boulangerie. With a touch of persuasion, he decided to dress in the semblance of a wiener würstchen, that esteemed Viennese delicacy which holds my favor. In the swirl of the fête, his chemically enhanced libidinous drive subconsciously steered him toward more fitting 'buns' to complement his 'meat,' sparking his transformation into a flirtatious tornado that wildly wooed the ladies at the party." While Chubata found mirth in his witticism, cracking a self-satisfied smirk, Grayus remained the epitome of solemn concentration. Chubata's expression shifted to one of grave solemnity as he proceeded with his exposition.

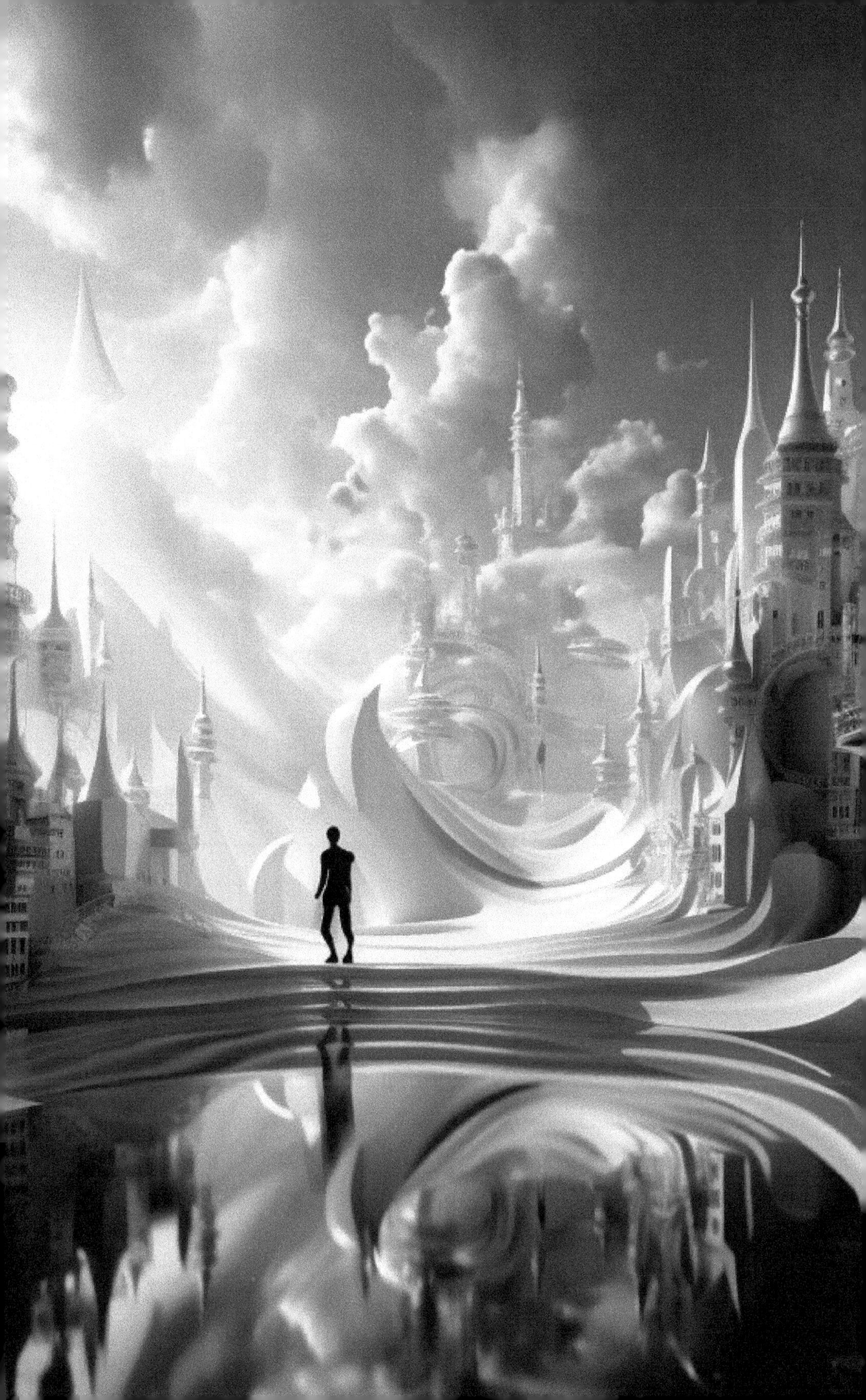

"My mission was to orchestrate their encounter at the perfect moment and location, a feat I achieved with aplomb. The subject became the epicenter of raucous laughter, drawing the party's attendees into a vortex of heavy flirting jests and gaiety. Witnessing this unsavory spectacle, his partner simmered with irritation yet maintained her composure. She made her way toward him and gave a gentle tap on his shoulder.

"Upon turning, his smile broadened as he quipped, 'My dear, you must be famished amidst this carnivorous feast...' This elicited uproarious laughter from the crowd.

"Armed with her sharp wit, she bided her time until the laughter subsided before retorting with a mix of humor and scorn, 'What a magnificent charcuterie soirée we're graced with today, adorned with such exquisite "meaty delights." Your foray into the culinary world of meat has always had my support. However, witnessing your relentless chase after mere "buns," loaded with an absurd amount of calories, has been more than I can stomach. This dietary debacle is where I draw the line; thus, I am leaving you. Goodbye!' His friends at the party attempted to suppress their laughter, feeling sympathy for their friend. She left the party with pride and soon after cut off all communication, creating an unbreakable barrier against his attempts to reach out." Chubata kept looking at Grayus's facial expression, trying to figure out his opinion on the report.

"The rupture of their tender connection was a testament to the dissolution of their intense chemical bond. This achievement verged on being a personal triumph for me, a seminal breakthrough in the realm of neurochemical manipulation of human-dolls. Yet, as I stood on the precipice of this success, a startling development unfolded, presenting itself as an unforeseen variable in my experimental odyssey." Chubata ceased speaking and moved toward the holographic screen to display the text for Grayus's review. He took his place beside the holographic display and thoughtfully addressed Grayus.

"Master, I implore you to peruse this document! It holds the quintessential proof underpinning the conclusion of my scholarly inquiry that I am about to present. Enclosed is her valedictory missive to him, a farewell document imbued with finality, sent to him after some time."

Grayus moved closer to the holographic screen and began to read the text:

*Your love was like the most beautiful butterfly.*
*Delightfully, it lifted me up to the mountains high!*
*My soul sang to your soul music,*
*Your soul joined mine—majestic!*

I opened up, and I could feel you around.
Tingling lights were like beautiful music sounds.
Were we supposed to become one?
If I ever LOVED this way, but none…

I became vulnerable to your surroundings.
I was coping, but a huge fear saw the door opening.
It overtook me by surprise!
It turned my love for you into demise.

You were close and witnessed me falling apart,
If ever one might think what a beautiful art.
It scared us both into rottenness.
You had developed a bad taste for my presence.

I fought and overcame my fear,
It was one for the mind, oh dear…
I have seen you with hundreds of eyes,
Not alone anymore with you otherwise.

The echoes of your words intertwined.
Your dreams were one with mine.
Extraordinaire, you pierced inside my heart.
I welcomed you happily—you became my ward!

Promises should have their keepers.
Many words flew away with glitters.
Beautiful lie turned into the ugly truth.
Let's just say we both might have a bruise.

*All sad stories stay away from us both,*
*The two happy kids following their dreams like moths.*
*If I can't be with you...*
*I WILL ALWAYS LOVE YOU!*

Grayus stopped perusing the document, and his eyes lifted to meet Chubata's. His gaze was punctuated by inquiry and contemplation.

"Indeed, you have caught my interest. Please continue your report."

The slight interest emanating from Grayus served as a reward for Chubata. He confidently positioned his arms behind his back and resumed his oration, infusing his delivery with a touch of theatrical flair.

"I hadn't anticipated any interaction between them, let alone a written correspondence, given that I had orchestrated events to wound them deeply. I must concede that occasionally, even to a being like myself, governed by meticulously calculated logic and cold, hard mathematics, the behavior of human-dolls can be startlingly unpredictable. When she composed this farewell poem, it was infused with a profound, lingering affection. Her words carried the weight of potent emotional memories, forging the neurochemical cues that once ignited their intense bond.

"It scarcely needs to be mentioned that when the male subject perused her goodbye note—an act of grandeur by the standards of human-doll conventions—it magnified the deliberate sentiment she had woven into the fabric of her words, ensuring that the emotional resonance would be deeply felt in its aftermath. The effect was nothing short of transformative; it excised the secondary anomaly, thus recalibrating the scales to balance his love for her and his family in equal measure. Such was the magnitude of this event that it not only expunged the secondary anomaly but also disrupted the entire communicative nexus between the assembly module and the control module responsible for mental manipulation. This led to an unequivocal dismantling of the manipulative and assimilative frameworks within the experimental subject."

It was as if the subject was roused from some farcical nightmare; the male human-doll bolted from the apartment, pursued comically by a few bourguignon aficionados who shrilly reminded him of his nearly non-existent attire. Unabashed, he dashed with ludicrous urgency to the abode of his former female companion. Upon her opening the door, intentsity of his gaze—charged with the raw emotion conveyed through her missive—acted as the final, integral piece of the puzzle. It was an anticipated yet profoundly cherished response that rekindled their love, reigniting a bond of affection now even more formidable than it was at its inception.

Chubata had to utilize the elite emergency response team to overhaul and replace the manipulation and absorption mechanisms within both dolls.

"In conclusion, despite the unforeseen complexities that arose, I maintain that the experiment confirmed the hypothesis that human-dolls, even when entrenched in deep emotional bonds, remain amenable to directed manipulation. This action depends on conducting manipulations within certain temporal frames, supported by scrupulous forecasting of the consequences of manipulative effects, all under the aegis of strict and methodical supervision. However, in the case of a very strong chemical bond, it will be necessary to use the emergency team, because manipulating such human-dolls is not possible." Chubata proudly finished and looked at Grayus with awe, awaiting his verdict. Grayus looked at him with an impenetrable look and deliberately paused. Then, his face burst into a happy, tearful smile. He slowly clapped his hands.

"I made no mistake by turning you into my faithful servant. You have worked too hard, and I want to give you a gift." Chubata's face lit up.

"We are going for a vacation at the best resort in Grayovius, to Vulcano del Chica. Put on some light clothes, my friend, cause this hot spot is very close to the Earth's core. However, the heat up there doesn't come from that." Grayus made a significant pause and then continued, laughing loudly.

"The heat comes from the spicy ladies!"

He approached Chubata, laughing, and patted him on the shoulder. The servant squeezed out a tortured smile; Grayus's laughter froze the blood in his veins.

# Chapter 27

# Psycho-Surfing

*I love psycho-surfing! An easier question to ask would be, what don't we do there? It's the best thing that the shmygs have come up with to stretch our imagination to the fullest and let off steam without violating our laws. Personally, I'm a big fan of psycho-surfing cafes. You can have fun with your friends and then have a discussion over delicious meals and drinks afterward.*

Smih Shmurk, GBC News

An unshaved, naked man in sneakers ran out onto the street and into the city center. His long, unwashed hair made him look like a Neanderthal. At the sight of his genitals swinging in all directions and overgrown with sprouts of abundant hair, every passerby bounced to the side in horror. He ran to the city market and stopped ten meters from the police patrol. He spread his legs wide, proudly rested his fists on his hips and stared at the police car with a brazen look, trying to catch their attention.

The policemen were sitting in a patrol car, peacefully eating their lunch. One of them caught a glimpse of the strange naked man. He poked his partner's elbow. Mouth full and burrito in his hand, the partner looked at him with discontent.

"Do you not see, Kenny? I'm eating my lunch! What!?" Josh, with a full mouth, turned his head in the direction of the naked man.

"Yes, but Josh, there is just a naked shit over here, brazenly staring at us!" They quickly finished their lunch and got out of the car.

As they approached the madman, Kenny took out a taser, and Josh unholstered his Glock 19. Both of them pointed their weapons at the naked man.

"Sir, please kneel and slowly put your hands behind your head," Josh commanded. Kenny turned to his partner and whispered softly.

"Josh, what the hell with the gun? He's naked!"

Josh looked at him with a hint of unhappiness and replied, "Maybe he hid a gun in his ass. Look at him. He's a crazy freak!"

When they turned their heads back toward the violator, his fists were pointed at them with their middle fingers drawn upward.

The hairy man smiled arrogantly at them as if saying, "I screwed you both, stupid underdog cops!"

The police officers glanced at him and, at the same time, as per command, holstered their weapons. As they took out rubber batons and slowly moved toward the naked man, his smile became even wider, and his facial expression conveyed a silent message:

"Try to catch up to me!"

It was as if a silent chase order was given, "March!"

All three of them rushed to the side of the vegetable stands in the city market. The hairy Neanderthal gained speed, ran to the first stand, and jumped onto a large table of tomatoes. He slid along the table on his naked behind, covering it with freshly squeezed tomato juice and wedging one tomato between his buttocks.

Jumping off the table, he cleverly snatched the semi-crushed tomato out from his inner-gluteal space and, without losing speed, turned around and threw it at the pursuer closest to him.

The tomato hit Josh directly in the eye, which distracted him for a moment and made him trip over the stool of one of the sellers. He tumbled all the way forward and crashed his head into the base of a pyramid of trays full of apples. The pyramid lost its balance and hit the officer over his head with all its mass.

The second police officer was not as fast as the first one due to his excessive weight. But after seeing his partner fall, he continued his pursuit of the tomato-butthead with a vengeance.

Without slowing down, the naked man shouted the battle cry of a Neanderthal, pulling his fist up and frightening all the sellers and buyers on his path. He spotted a small pickup truck loaded with rotten vegetables and fruits driving away from the shopping area. He caught up to it and jumped inside like a diving fish. Only his red tomato butt remained on the surface.

Breathing heavily, the second police officer stopped, bent over, and leaned his hands on his knees. The officer helplessly watched his prey escape; the prey's middle finger was rising alongside his tomato butt from the rotten produce.

# Chapter 28

# A Nervous Breakdown

*The perception of an individual is shaped in such a way that, at any given moment, a main object stands out while everything else fades into the background. However, the paradox lies in the fact that this main object is often greatly exaggerated, hindering our ability to discern the background. This background, perhaps, holds the answers to many of our questions.*

Dr. Fritz Pörlez, GBC News Interview

In the office of the detective at the Lower Level district police, Chubata sat with a bruise under his eye, reeking of strong alcohol, grimy and in torn clothes, and with his head lowered. A young shmyg police lieutenant smoked a cigarette as he slowly drew up a protocol. A sleepless night left traces of fatigue on his face, and he sipped on a cold cup of coffee.

"Tell me again, how did you get to the Lower Level?" He looked carefully at the brawler sitting in front of him and exhaled a big puff of smoke in his direction.

Chubata slowly raised his head, looked indifferently at the detective, involuntarily burped, and spoke indignantly in a drunken voice interrupted by hiccups.

"My master promised me—hic-hic—Vulcano del Chica, mother f—hic-hic—after all, I am!" He hit himself hard with his fist in the chest.

"I worked like a damned one, his mother f—hic-hic-hic."

Chubata looked confidently at the officer as if he would tell him some kind of secret, then bent a little and quietly spoke in a conspiratorial voice.

"Do you understand? Hic-hic. I went to him, and I asked my master when we would go to the resort, to the chicks—hic-hic—Oh, do you know what he answered?" Chubata looked at the detective significantly, as if they were sitting at a table in a bar drinking together, discussing all his troubles. The police officer carelessly shrugged, playing along, and took a small sip of cold coffee.

Chubata involuntarily reached out with his hand for a drink, then realized he was no longer in the bar and put his hand back. Again, he spoke loudly and indignantly.

"He told me to know my place, mother f—hic-hic—like I didn't deserve to have fun with chicks. I—!" One more time, he hit himself hard in the chest, his face took on an ominous expression, and he screamed, with all his voice, instantly raging.

"It is I!—hic-hic—for two hundred years, I kept the entire surface of the globe in fear, I ruled the world, I created the greatest rulers in the history of human-dolls. No one dared to disrespect me! That's why, when this asshole in the strip bar called me a gnome, I hit him in the face—hic-hic." Suddenly, as if intoxicated again, he smiled and looked good-naturedly at the officer.

"Take you, for example. You respect me—hic-hic—and me too. Buddy, it is so good that you and I have met—hic-hic—give me another cup—hic-hic."

The officer looked incredulously at the tatterdemalion shmyg. He could not understand what he was talking about.

"Which rulers? What master? Who is he? He is not in any database!"

Someone quietly knocked on the door of the office, and another officer stepped inside. After an approving nod from the young lieutenant officer, he approached the table from his side with a folder in his hands. The police officers flicked the folder while whispering and throwing startled glances at Chubata. Finally, the second officer exited, leaving the folder behind.

He looked incredulously at the rowdy shmyg and said in a strict voice, "Does the name Shpik Chubatius tell you something?"

Suddenly, Chubata jolted sharply as if his brain had been pricked with a needle from the inside. He knew this name very well but could not remember where or when he might have heard it. The neural connections of his psycho-correction took his thoughts in another direction, not allowing him to focus, like a crowd of cheerful gypsies taking an onlooker aside. But it felt so familiar, as if it were his native name.

"Who is that?" asked Chubata, sincerely interested.

The officer looked at him with surprise and admiration for the brawler's acting skills and replied victoriously, "A DNA test confirmed that it was you!"

He showed him the test results. Once again, Chubata's train of thought unexpectedly swerved. The officer wondered whether he was interrogating a drug addict. Although Chubata was pretty drunk, he was still a professional—he created a mental safe where he put the information he had just received. It was very important to him.

Loud steps came down the corridor, and three Grayovius secret police officers entered the office without knocking. The most important among them approached the table unceremoniously, handed a piece of paper to the young officer, and spoke arrogantly.

"We're taking over this case due to the special importance of the Council of the Ancients. All available records, personal files, samples, and other materials are seized by personal order of the director of the secret police. You and anyone else are forbidden to discuss details of what you have learned. In accordance with Directive 548-GC, all violators face the death penalty without trial." The secret police officer looked strictly at the young officer from top to bottom. The young officer shrank, paralyzed with fear, and nodded.

Two of the secret police officers handcuffed Chubata and put a black bag over his head. All four quickly left the Lower Level district police building. The fleeting gypsy-thoughts kept circling in Chubata's head. No one suspected that there was "a mental safe with very important information" right under their noses.

# Chapter 29

# The Secret Police

*The secret of life, though, is to fall seven times and to get up eight times.*

Paulo Coelho

The transport capsule delivered its passengers to their destination in minutes. Three high-ranking agents escorted Chubata through several levels of admission to the director's office in the main directorate of the secret police. They unlocked his handcuffs and removed the black bag from his head. Chubata wanted to look around, but he was forcibly turned toward a door and pushed inside a room.

The door closed, and Chubata found himself in a large office with a long conference table and chairs.

Someone hidden by a shadow sat at the head of the table in a very large chair. The dim light in the room illuminated his pipe.

The pipe sputtered loudly, and a stranger at the table blew a large tangle of toroidal smoke toward Chubata, leaving a strong aroma of flavored tobacco as it dissipated. Chubata involuntarily inhaled the remains of the smoke with his nostrils, remembering frequent visits to hookah bars in his youth.

From the shadow emerged a huge, humped nose and a wide-smiling face. It was Grayus. Anger rushed through Chubata as he realized his master was the director of the secret police of Grayovius.

"Did you like the Lower Level?" asked Grayus kindly.

Chubata, feeling guilty because he had fled from his workplace by deceiving the security on several floors, fearfully replied in a small voice.

"It was fun at the strip bar, at first... and then, I don't remember well."

Grayus again disappeared into the shadows and blew another cloud of smoke toward Chubata. Chubata wanted to ask Grayus about the name he heard from the young officer but intuitively knew it was better not to ask.

"I have a very hard job, my friend." Grayus continued suddenly in a half-asleep voice.

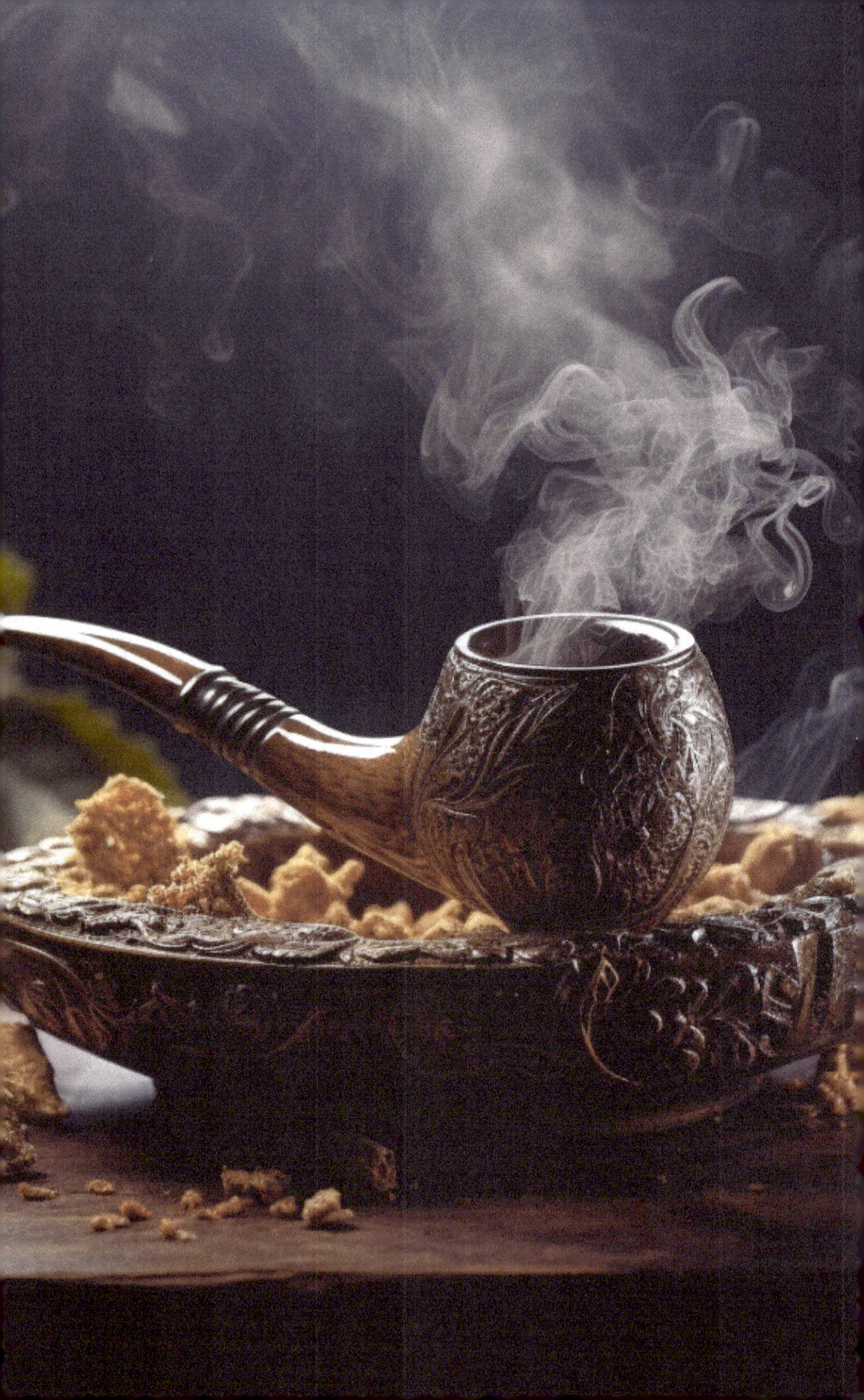

"Recruitment, surveillance, wiretapping, external surveillance, collection of incriminating information on everyone, especially on those who have power. Agent networks, cells of unspoken agents, appearances, passwords, elimination of unsuitable authorities, counterintelligence activities, and any such secret shit. You have no idea how tired I am. I guess I should have taken you to Vulcano del Chica. Yes, it would not hurt to get some rest myself. However, I am constantly in a hurry somewhere because I want to please the Council. Although, I have huge folders of compromising evidence for each of the Ancients."

Grayus paused his tangent and continued in a whisper.

"I know the young officer told you something. But trust me, what he said makes no sense. Come to me."

He summoned Chubata with his hand. Chubata came closer fearfully, and Grayus turned his huge smoking pipe's mouthpiece to him.

"**Drag on!**" Grayus commanded. Chubata put the pipe in his mouth, took a big puff, and lost consciousness.

# Chapter 30

# The Resort

*Vulcano del Chica is an absolutely accurate copy of the Musha Cay resort from the surface of the Earth. We have done tremendous work; you will not even realize that you are right under the Himalayas, forty five miles deep.*

Principal Architect,
Underground Construction, Inc.,
GBC News Interview

Chubata slept soundly on his stomach atop a soft massage table on the largest beach at the Vulcano del Chica resort. High above him, the artificial sun shone brightly, pleasantly warming his skin with ultraviolet light. A masseuse in a bikini slowly massaged his neck and shoulders. Chubata suddenly woke up, sharply raised his head, and frantically looked around. He did not understand how he found himself here, but he really liked this place—and the masseuse. He put his head back down on the towel and relaxed.

He turned his head to a more comfortable position and noticed a note lying right in front of his nose. Without changing the position of his body, he carefully opened it with one hand and read it to himself.

Dear Chubata,

I am sorry! I was wrong when I promised you a holiday at the resort and did not fulfill my promise. You really did a great job and earned this vacation like no other. Unfortunately, I can't be there because of matters of national importance, but I think the smoking chicks will soothe your loneliness and you will have a wonderful time. A limitless doll-coin card is in the left pocket of your shorts.

Enjoy your two-week vacation. I can't give more time for your rest.

Respectfully,
G.

Chubata delicately put the note in his pocket. He was at the absolute maximum on the scale of happiness; at last, his master appreciated his talents. His thoughts flashed in his head like butterflies, and he did not notice the loss of the mental safe with very important information...

# Chapter 31

# Hibernation

*The use of artificial hibernation is illegal throughout Grayovius. Many claim that our secret police use this barbaric method to carry out unauthorized manipulations of shmygs to this day. However, I assure you that it is not true.*

Chief Prosecutor of Grayovius,<br>GBC News Interview

For three months now, Chubata had been in a state of artificial hibernation in one of many special capsules at a secret military base. The hangar where he slept was filled with the latest equipment in the field for consciousness correction and manipulation. Scientists with the highest level of security clearance for state secrets worked there, equipped with the latest technology.

A high-ranking official entered the hangar, and all the scientists, as if according to an unspoken command, stretched along the counter. Accompanied by personal protection, he slowly approached capsule 3b, in which Chubata was located. He addressed the scientist officer on duty in a good-natured tone.

"How are things going with my friend?"

Although the question was rather vague, the officer realized everything should be reported, including minor details. He took a close look at the monitor, stood up straight as a pole, and reported in a clear voice.

"The object C., according to your personal instructions, is in a state of happiness, so to speak, at the resort. He has been there for five days. In real-time, he has been in a state of hibernation for ninety-one days, six hours, and thirty-five minutes. During hibernation, he received a full scan of neural connections, memory, and the motivational vector of the object. A change in his memory at the cellular level was carried out. The key psycho-neuronic connections were redirected, and the motivation vector was adjusted in accordance with your technical assignment. The estimated time to complete the manipulation is seventy-two hours. When the object regains consciousness, he will consider you his own father. He will love you with all his heart and unquestionably abide by all your orders." Grayus's face lit up with a smile—the same as the smile of happy fathers.

# Chapter 32

# The Father

*Happiness is the state of an individual characterized by the highest internal satisfaction with their life conditions, sense of completeness, and the fulfillment of their calling and self-realization.*

The Greatest Largest Shmygopedia

Chubata woke up in his room to the loud chirping of birds outside the window. It was wide open, and soft artificial sunlight penetrated inside. Not everyone could afford artificial sun, but in their family estate, it was almost always present ever since Chubata was very young and his father received an important public office.

He did not remember his mother's face at all, although his memories of that fateful day were very well preserved. His father told him the tragic news of her death due to a faulty transportation capsule. He cried a lot that day, realizing his powerlessness to turn back time and prevent the accident.

For as long as Chubata could remember, he had always studied a lot. He graduated from more than fifty prestigious universities in Grayovius and received doctorate degrees and academic degrees in more than a hundred advanced areas of science. For the last two hundred years, he taught the course on the resonant quasi-spatial branch of the time loop at the Grayovius State Academy as a professor of the faculty of incomplete studies.

His main research work was devoted to creating a time-lapse device in a controlled time loop. He felt that his brain was like a huge supercomputer. He knew thousands of scientific works and research papers in this field by heart. It was as if a huge suitcase of advanced developments of shmygs were put in his brain.

He felt a little dizzy and rose to sit on the bed. He could not get used to his huge, humped nose, although he'd had it since birth.

Chubata's malaise disappeared as quickly as it had appeared, and he hurried to his father's gazebo in the garden. In the morning hours, his favorite spot was often there. On his way, several gardeners bowed to him in a cordial greeting. At the gazebo, he saw his father and his heart was filled with trepidation. He ran to his father with all his speed, crying out joyfully.

"Dad!"

The guard respectfully stepped aside to let him in as Chubata approached the gazebo. Grayus turned around, smiling as tears welled in his eyes.

"Son!"

Chubata clung to his father with both hands, pressed his head against his chest, and did not let go for a long time. Chubata's father was the most valuable and closest living creature to him in the whole world.

Finally, they sat down in their rocking chairs and picked up their smoking pipes. Almost simultaneously, they both took deep puffs. Their tubes spluttered pleasantly, sending huge portions of smoke into their lungs. After the first puff, the humps on their noses pulsated and tingled, sending impulses of pleasure into their bodies.

They simultaneously leaned into their chairs, looked up to the gazebo's ceiling, and released huge toroidal clouds of smoke that slowly rose to the ceiling together and dissolved without a trace. They took a second, even stronger puff and held their breath for a moment. They released all the smoke through their noses and, for a moment, disappeared in it. They resembled two locomotives releasing excess steam through their safety valves. Something made them both laugh very hard at the same time. Chubata loved his father's laughter, and his father liked Chubata's laughter. All the gardeners at the greenhouse shrank with horror, hearing this loud double laugh at the same time. Even the thunderbolt guards at the entrance hesitantly began to move their feet in fear.

The father and son were in a state of absolute happiness. They took a third, even more powerful puff and plunged into a deep sleep.

# Chapter 33

# The Experiment

*Embrace the courage to push your boundaries, because it is by venturing into the unknown that we acquire knowledge and evolve.*

Baltz Wisniewski's Personal Journal

Baltz made a new batch of honey krupnik in full secrecy. His wife did not hear a whisper. He removed the wormwood from his new recipe, fearing it could affect the final product's quality. However, his fears were in vain.

He dipped his index finger in a bottle, held it a little in the air, and smelled it seductively as if it were a freshly fried Polish sausage. He stuck his entire finger into his mouth and licked it, trying to catch the different notes and aromas.

Then he froze like a statue, holding the three-liter bottle firmly with both hands. Tormented doubts burst into his mind. Glancing at the clock from the corners of his eyes, he saw it was 7:20 in the morning. Baltz lifted the bottle in front of him for a closer look, as if handling a newborn baby. The morning sun penetrated the basement's small window, passed through the bottle, and shone on everything around with amber light.

Baltz's torment came to an end, and he took a large sip of what he called "the shining tears of a baby" from the bottle. The honey krupnik spread a pleasant warmth throughout his body, and he noted with satisfaction that removing the wormwood did not diminish the liquor's bright and rich taste.

From above, he heard the impatient and irritated voice of his wife.

"Baltz! What are you digging yourself into, old fool? Did you fix the iron press?"

He hastily put the bottle into a secret hiding place and, having eaten a salted cucumber and a dill twig to disguise the smell of alcohol, took an iron press and ran upstairs. After subduing his wife's vigilance, he returned downstairs, quickly bottled the krupnik, slipped one bottle into a spacious inner pocket of his jacket, and shouted, "I am off to the railway station," before leaving the house.

He arrived at the town park by 7:30 a.m., where he and his young, only friend, Karl, had agreed to meet at a specific tree. Although krupnik always brought ease and fun, the main goal of today's experiment was to refute their hallucinations from a couple of days earlier.

Karl stood alone in dark sunglasses, carelessly leaning against the tree. He resembled a secret agent trying too hard to conceal his identity. Baltz approached Karl directly and walked past him as if he were a stranger. Karl, committed to the art of stealth, quietly followed. The friends then made their way to a secluded meadow surrounded by bushes, choosing a spot that shielded them from view on all sides. Without a word, Baltz produced the bottle, and Karl retrieved a snack from his pants pocket, everything arranged as per the plan they'd made the previous day. Their modest feast included two boiled potatoes, a few slices of sausage, two cucumbers, a small piece of dried pig's fat, salo, and a generous bunch of dill.

Baltz squinted cleverly, extended his hands forward, and performed a subtle, fluid movement with his entire body. Shortly thereafter, a pair of small iron cups materialized in his hands, marking his signature magic trick. With pride, he placed the cups on a makeshift table. Sighing in relief, he filled the krupnik to the brim, with the liquid glittering in the sunlight. Today, the friends felt no pangs of conscience for indulging in a morning drink.

Without any guilt, they proudly raised their cups. Instead of feeling like alcoholics, they saw themselves as pioneering scientists or adventurous experimenters, volunteering to test an unknown medicine to save lives. They both quickly drained their cups in one go. Exhaling to relax, they settled more comfortably on the grass. Baltz showed two fingers, and Karl immediately grasped the gesture's meaning.

"Between the first and the second, the break is small," said Baltz.

Baltz refilled the cups, and with the same pride and selflessness as before, they downed the contents. Smiles appeared on their faces, and Baltz deliberately began to speak in a grandiloquent manner.

"My kind and honorable friend, Karl! Please, let me introduce you to a new and improved version of my divine drink, which causes absolutely no hallucinations."

He gestured toward the bottle of krupnik with his hands, as if introducing Karl to an unfamiliar and venerable lady. Karl played along, theatrically extending and squeezing his right hand in the air and bowing his head as though greeting this imaginary lady. "I've heard so much about you, my respected madam!" Barely holding back his laughter, Karl continued, "I will be very pleased to drink you all the way to the bottom, together with my friend!"

They both burst into loud laughter. Karl stretched out on the grass, placing his hands under his head.

"Truly, our troubles have come to an end! It's unbelievable that all this happened because of a mere pinch of wormwood!"

He sat up sharply and looked at Baltz with admiration.

"Let's drink to you, my dear Baltz! This research—and I do not hesitate to use that word—has undoubtedly succeeded!"

Baltz squared his shoulders and proudly poured another round, which they immediately downed. The morning was simply wonderful, with the two buddies enjoying lively conversation, merrily drinking one glass after another.

Suddenly, from behind the bushes, loud, humorous laughter erupted. A silent question hung in their eyes: 'Had someone else decided to arrange an impromptu picnic in the park?'

It was highly unusual, prompting both of them to slowly crawl toward the bushes to investigate. Peering through the foliage, they caught a glimpse of a large table lavishly laden with exotic dishes and drinks. At the table sat two young individuals, a man and a woman, both dressed in unconventional attire, accompanied by two cats also clad in whimsical outfits. All four solemnly raised glasses filled with sparkling drinks. The young man then lifted his glass higher and cheerfully proposed a toast.

"Here's to our dear Lea! Cheers to her birthday! While it's not customary to talk about a woman's age, since she has now lived 141,000 years, it's certainly worth mentioning!"

Everyone joyfully raised their glasses and was about to drink when the woman stopped them and addressed everyone at the table.

"Thank you so much for such flattering words! However, we are missing two more guests at our table today, whom I mentioned yesterday when we were planning this picnic. These chairs were specially prepared for them."

She nodded her head toward the empty seats.

Baltz and Karl listened intently, their jaws dropping in astonishment. They kept their eyes fixed on the scene, as if paralyzed by the spectacle.

"I think our guests need our help to be seated at the table." The woman took a napkin from the table and softly waved it in the air. Suddenly, Baltz and Karl found themselves sitting at the table, with glasses in their hands, having no understanding of how that had happened.

"Now we can drink!" The woman said joyfully, clinking her glass with theirs.

The expressions on Karl's and Baltz's faces had not changed since they were in the bushes, watching everything from the outside. Their unusual company emptied their glasses; Baltz and Karl followed them, without any understanding of what they were doing.

They drank everything, and when they finished, their faces expressed mute delight.

"Délicieux!" Karl unexpectedly exclaimed in French, with an accent typical of the northeastern Champenois dialect. Startled, he quickly covered his mouth with his hand, bewildered by his newfound knowledge of the language.

"Do not be afraid, my dear friend," the woman said, kindly tapping his shoulder. "You've just had champagne made from a special variety of grapes that grow in the northeastern Champagne region of France."

Baltz looked at the black cat with wonder, not taking his eyes off him. Finally, the cat could not stand such a curious gaze and indignantly addressed the guest.

"Sir, of course, you are a guest at this party, but please do not look at me as if I were a dumb animal." He proudly lifted his muzzle.

"By the way, I am the only cat with a doctorate in philosophy!"

Baltz's jaw dropped even lower. The young man promptly decided to intervene to prevent his complete stupor.

"I have a beautiful drink, which our guest will appreciate!"

He took a small bottle with a bright purple hue and filled the guests' glasses to the edges.

Baltz drained the glass with a salvo, and his eyes filled with pleasure. He spoke quickly, with gestures like an inveterate Italian.

"Questa bevanda è semplicemente divina. Ringrazio il destino per essere allo stesso tavolo con i miei cari amici!" Baltz was so surprised by his speech that he dropped the glass on the ground and covered his mouth with both hands.

"My dear, thank you! Beautifully spoken. Let me translate what you have just said: 'This drink is just divine. I thank fate for being at the same table with my dear friends!'" She laughed happily.

"This is the best birthday present ever! I think it's time for our guests to go to sleep because what will happen next is very dangerous for their health!" She laughed again and waved her handkerchief.

Suddenly, it was late evening, and Baltz and Karl were sleeping peacefully in the meadow. The remnants of their snacks were scattered around, with the empty bottle of krupnik lying in the middle. They woke up almost simultaneously, looked at each other with incredulity, and quickly ran home, driven by fear.

# Chapter 34

# The Hangover

*A hangover in humans results from consuming excessive alcohol, and is characterized by discomfort and symptoms such as headaches, irritability, dry mouth, sweating, and nausea. Prolonged heavy drinking over several days can also cause auditory and visual hallucinations.*

Amandine's Personal Journal

The next morning was, to say the least, not good. Baltz and Karl sat silently on a bench next to the railway station, the aftermath visible on their faces. A black eye was a stark feature on Baltz's face, a souvenir from his wife. Being a formidable woman, she had not taken kindly to him returning home reeking of alcohol, and had promptly rewarded his drunken state with a solid punch to the eye. Karl's ordeal was no less severe;

his ear, bright red and slightly protruding, bore the marks of his mother's wrath. She had dragged him by the ear like a schoolboy, hurling swear words at him in full view of their neighbors.

The experiment had failed disastrously, and their situation had significantly worsened. Confusion reigned, and neither could fathom their next steps. On one hand, acknowledging the reality of what they had witnessed seemed an express route to madness; no one would ever believe their story. On the other hand, to deny it would be to live in dishonesty with themselves. Faced with such a choice, embracing madness seemed the lesser of two evils.

Curiosity and fear plagued them. The steam locomotive was supposed to be in the depot for another week for annual maintenance, giving them ample free time. They exchanged silent looks before suddenly rising to inspect the site of yesterday's feast. They hoped to find evidence confirming that everything they had seen the day before was not a hallucination.

When they came back to the small meadow, the empty bottle of krupnik still lay on the ground. Baltz slipped the empty bottle into his inner pocket, thinking it might still be of use. Karl collected the remains of their snack and threw them into the nearest garbage container. The two friends felt a little better after cleaning up the place. They looked at each other anxiously and approached the ill-fated site of the picnic.

When they leaned out of the bushes, they simultaneously experienced fear and relief. In front of them, just as they remembered, was the huge table and chairs, now empty. When they got closer, they saw two glasses and a small bottle filled with some incredible liquid, transfused with bright amber-yellow colors and moving as if alive. A note sat beside the bottle. Baltz read it aloud.

Dear friends,

We are deeply grateful for your presence with us yesterday. Please be assured, we are not a figment of your imagination, just as you are not a figment of ours. We regret that you couldn't stay with us until the celebration's end. However, in gratitude for the joy you brought us, we're leaving you this magical potion. It will cure your hangover and reveal all the events you missed after our unfortunate parting. We wish you a delightful and enchanting viewing experience!

Kindly,
Your guardians

Baltz put the note aside and lightly slapped himself on the cheeks. Karl's face was a little pale, but curiosity burned in his eyes. They sat at the table, and Baltz, as the more senior of the two of them, fearfully poured the magical liquid into the glasses. Both friends took the glasses in their hands and looked at each other with doom as if they were saying goodbye. After a short pause, they drank all of it.

They experienced a bliss they had never felt before. It was as though they had instantly uncovered all the secrets of the universe, like two innocent babies. Their souls were calmer than ever as their eyes closed slowly, and they fell into a deep, restful sleep.

# Chapter 35

# A Dream Within A Dream

*Dreaming involves the subjective perception of images—visual, auditory, tactile, gustatory, and olfactory—that emerge in the consciousness of a sleeping human-doll. On average, a human-doll spends about twenty-three years of their life sleeping, with eight of those years dedicated to dreaming.*

*The Greatest Largest Shmygopedia*

*Take this kiss upon the brow!*
*And, in parting from you now,*
*Thus much let me avow —*
*You are not wrong, who deem*
*That my days have been a dream;*
*Yet if hope has flown away*
*In a night, or in a day,*
*In a vision, or in none,*
*Is it therefore the less gone?*
*All that we see or seem*
*Is but a dream within a dream.*

Edgar Allan Poe,
"A Dream Within A Dream"

As Karl and Baltz dreamed, they seemed to watch everything from an external perspective. They observed themselves sitting at the table with that peculiar company, then saw their bodies rise into the air and gently descend onto the meadow where they had awoken the previous day. Meanwhile, the company continued to revel and offer toasts without them. Remarkably, most toasts were proposed by a black cat, who had introduced himself as a doctor of philosophy.

Suddenly, the young man's watch emitted a strange sound. He looked at everyone and urgently announced that they were being summoned by the Great Intergalactic Council to the planet Galanthus. Instantly, all four guardians transformed into luminous spheres and soared upward at incredible speed. Baltz and Karl pursued them, moving faster than they had ever experienced before.

They left Earth's atmosphere and rushed into outer space, accelerating even faster and passing hundreds of thousands of galaxies and billions of planets. It seemed that they were moving to the other end of the universe. Finally, they slowed down as they approached a huge planet that looked a little like Earth, but twice as big.

A disembodied voice explained to them that they were on the planet Galanthus. This planet was part of a symbiosis of two solar systems that featured a complex network of orbital paths. As a result, the planet never experienced night; the sunrise from one sun perpetually replaced the sunset of the other.

As they landed, they encountered many outlandish buildings—some of which literally reached the sky. Approaching the surface, they observed extraordinary living beings. Some bore a resemblance to humans, but most appeared strikingly idiosyncratic, beyond the descriptive powers of Baltz and Karl. These fantastic, intelligent lifeforms were unlike anything they had ever seen.

Eventually, they approached a vast and fascinating structure that resembled a massive stadium from above. They entered through an opening at the top and made their way to a special area near a structure akin to a stage. At its heart, a colossal toad-like creature—five times larger than the Grayville railway station house—was perched on a silver platform. She was surrounded by stadium tiers brimming with approximately one and a half million indescribable beings from various species. The tiers ascended so high they appeared to reach the sky.

The four luminous spheres advanced to a silver platform directly in front of the toad. As if by a magician's wave, a fifth luminous sphere promptly joined them—it was the fifth guardian, Regea. The incredible noise from the vast crowd ceased. The glowing shells dissolved without a trace, revealing five beings from Septarion standing before the assembly. The huge toad-like creature addressed the audience.

"I would like to remind everyone gathered here that, in accordance with the Charter of Liberties, each convocation of the Great Intergalactic Council—which convenes here out of absolute necessity—includes two randomly selected life forms from every galaxy within the Bequest Community of Galaxies. As the permanent Scribe of the Great Intergalactic Council, I possess no voting rights but am solely tasked with articulating its decisions."

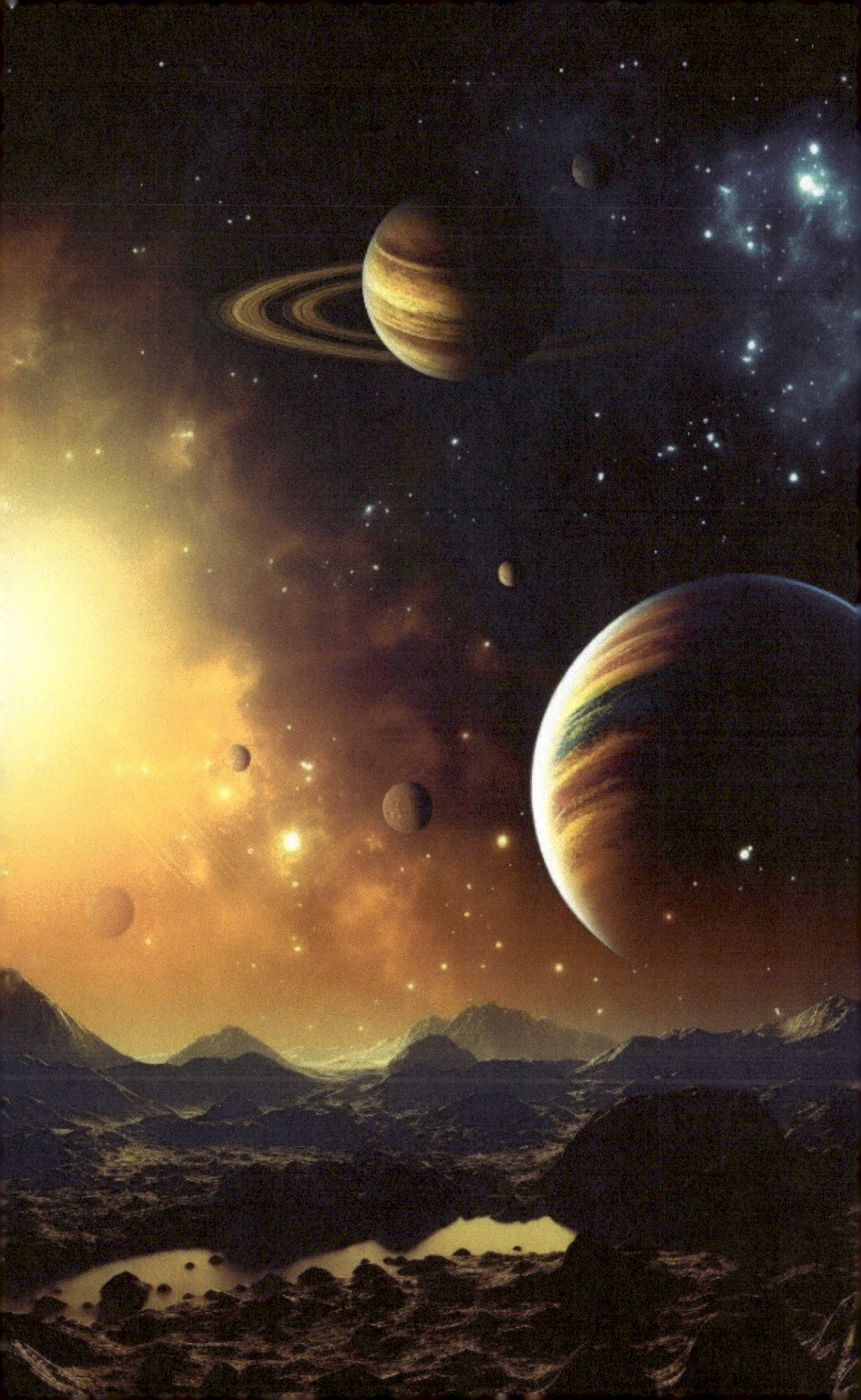

Beside the enormous toad-like creature sat a smaller counterpart, roughly the size of their steam locomotive. The smaller creature rose on the silver platform to whisper something into the ear of the larger one. The sound of the whispering was similar to a light breeze. The huge toad-like creature continued.

"My assistant scribe informed me that today there are 2,987,654 representatives gathered from almost one and a half million galaxies in the Bequest Community of the Galaxies."

She paused for a moment, then pointed one of her six limbs toward the newly arrived party.

"Our guardians have completed their investigative mission on planet Ambassador, a world engulfed in wars and on the brink of self-destruction!"

A hum of discontent swept through the rows. After a moment, the scribe addressed the five young Septarioneons.

"Dear Guardians, kindly share the results of your investigation."

One of the five guardians came forward. She waited until the noise of the crowd subsided and spoke confidently.

"My name is Lea, and I serve as the chief guardian of the Stellar Sentinel, *Synus*. Together with my fellow guardians, we have conducted a thorough investigation, revealing that this planet has experienced its third sowing attempt. The prior two sowing efforts resulted in destruction. In our quest to identify common factors behind these failures, we discovered that during the initial sowing, the chief agrobiologist of the Bequest Community of the Galaxies, for reasons yet to be understood, introduced a species alongside the humans. This species, known as the underground shmyg, exhibits a propensity for violence and is explicitly banned under the Convention of Safe Sowing."

A loud murmur of unease swept through the hall, growing into a buzz of indignation, until the big scribe was forced to intervene. The colossal toad-like creature screamed.

"Quiet!"

At that moment, all the walls on planet Earth shook for a moment.

The crowd quieted down, and Lea continued.

"Each time we destroyed the unsuccessful sowing, we did not destroy the shmygs because they were deep underground. Resorting to manipulation and correction of consciousness, they constantly waged wars on the surface of the unfortunate trial planet, which, in the end, led to the destruction of another sowing on our part. Evolution and long life have enabled these creepers to make incredible advances in science, and they are practically just a step away from creating a device to control consciousness in a time loop. This is already a threat to the entire Bequest Community of the Galaxies!" The buzz of indignation became even louder, and the big scribe had to intervene again.

"The chief agrobiologist is invited to testify!"

The chief agrobiologist glided to the center of the hall on a large silver platform. Resembling a huge turtle, he continuously puffed on a giant hookah, emitting smoke clouds in intricate shapes. With a release of smoke shaped like a four-masted sailboat, he raised one flipper and began to speak slowly.

"I am the chief agrobiologist of the Bequest Community of the Galaxies, and I swear on the Charter of Liberties that I will tell the truth and nothing but the truth."

After completing the oath and taking another puff, the creature that looked like a turtle released a smoke cloud shaped like Earth and began to speak in a leisurely tone.

"We found this planet in the unexplored sector 54378-GT. That day, I smoked a lot of smoking mixtures, which I take constantly for inspiration. I think that is why, when entering introductory genetic data, I accidentally duplicated the code of prohibited sowing material and added to the sowing one of the plants that was the basis for my medicine. I admit my mistake."

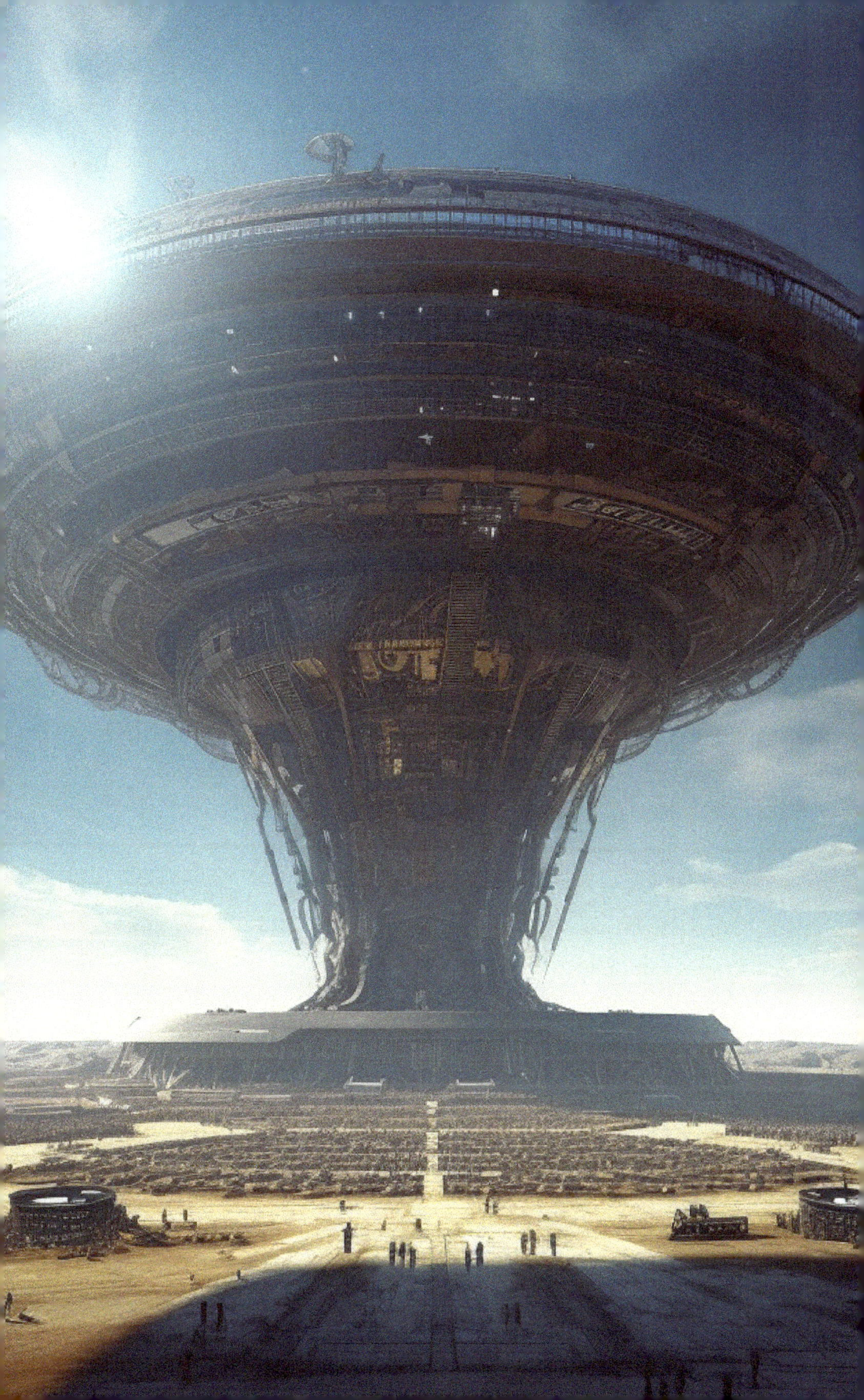

A hum of disapproval swept through the hall again. The big scribe loudly asked the chief agrobiologist, "Please specify which plant and which gene code you have added?"

The turtle-like creature took a puff and released a swirl of smoke depicting a shmyg holding a branch of some plant in its hands.

"I admit, I have added *Shmygus Infestantibus* and *Tabacum Magicum*."

A powerful wave of anger covered the hall as almost three million living beings loudly protested at the same time. Finally, when the noise of the crowd quieted down, the big scribe spoke calmly.

"In accordance with the Charter of Liberties of the Bequest Community of the Galaxies, any punishment is prohibited. Everyone is their own judge. Thus, from the bottom of our hearts, we pardon you with full forgiveness!"

A buzz of general approval and applause swept through the hall. The turtle took a deep puff and released a huge tangle of smoke in the shape of Galanthus and its two suns. He bowed to the hall and retired back to his box as leisurely as he had flown to the center.

Lea spoke again. "Before the Council makes a decision on this beautiful planet, let me present to you the living proof. This being was sentenced to execution, but we saved him right from the hands of death. He told us many interesting facts and contributed to the investigation."

A portal materialized in the center of another platform adjacent to the guardians', and Tiberius emerged, as terrified as a small mouse. Though he was accustomed to vast stadiums, he had never before encountered such a diversity of beings in one place. Gazing at the huge toad-like being, he was seized by fear, convinced he had been summoned to be its meal.

The big scribe, having discerned the thoughts of the diminutive shmyg, laughed heartily with her entire being. In that instant, the walls of planet Earth trembled once again.

"He thinks I will eat him!" she said through tears of laughter.

Everyone joined in millions of different shades of laughter: screeching, grunting, shaking, muttering, rustling, buzzing, and many more.

The big scribe asked Tiberius quietly and gently after everyone had laughed heartily, "Please, tell us about yourself, little guy."

Tiberius proudly tossed his head at her and began to speak confidently.

"In my world, I'm not a little guy. By our standards, I'm a giant! I am a famous champion and the only shmyg trapper who was able to pacify the dream quadro-matter."

The whole hall shone with admiration.

"Of course, of course, please forgive me!" Said the huge toad-like creature politely.

"I have not seen *Shmygus Infestantibus* for a long time and had turned away from your warlike morals. Yes, I congratulate you! I think you're an outstanding shmyg within your kind."

The big scribe shrugged and continued to the next main article of the convocation of the Great Intergalactic Council.

"Who is in favor of cleansing from all forms of life on planet Ambas—"

She was interrupted by a figure emerging from the shadows, who addressed the assembly loudly and excitedly.

"Please, stop!"

At that moment, everyone in the hall, including the scribes, froze, and absolute silence enveloped Earth.

A man with short red hair, a mustache, and a beard glided into the hall's center on his silver platform. He was dressed in a cyan jacket, white shirt, black waistcoat, black pants, and brown shoes. A bright blue butterfly sat on his left shoulder: *Morpho Amathonte.*

He halted the platform just in front of the Great Intergalactic Council's chief scribe, offering a smile to those around him as he awaited permission to speak.

The colossal toad-like creature regarded him with a smile and then addressed him respectfully.

Widba, the adults will educate you, but in doing so, you might miss the truth.

"Dear Supreme Observer, you, like no other, should be well aware that interrupting the vote of the Great Intergalactic Council is not allowed. However, because of the seriousness of the matter, I will ask the Council to vote on your right to speak."

The sounds of voting buttons being pressed filled the hall as the Great Intergalactic Council concluded the vote. The assistant scribe then presented the voting results to the toad.

After some time, the chief scribe of the Council announced the decision calmly.

"Dear Supreme Observer, you are invited to speak. Please elaborate on the reason for your appearance."

Supreme Observer calmly began to speak.

"I swear by the Charter of Liberties to tell the truth, the whole truth, and nothing but the truth. I had the honor of being appointed as the Supreme Observer of the trial planet Ambassador from its very inception. I have closely monitored this planet, observing the development of the humans as well as the progression of the banned species, *Shmygus Infestantibus*.

"The truth is, the shmygs have taught humans a great deal and have been instrumental in their development across all areas. They introduced new knowledge to the humans, aiding in their early progress. This is the reason I refrained from summoning the guardians of the Bequest Community of the Galaxies for an extended period.

"The most dire consequence of the underground shmygs manipulating human consciousness was the eradication of the humans' free will, which adversely impacted their development by not aligning with their best interests. If the Great Intergalactic Council grants me permission to employ a long forgotten technique and pollinate the planet Ambassador with *Pulvis Iridis*[3], reaching even its deepest underground regions—then the *Shmygus Infestantibus* will transform into a new species, *Shmygus Humanus*. I am convinced that this new symbiosis will unlock tremendous positive potential. I implore you to authorize this symbiosis and thereby save the inhabitants of the trial planet Ambassador."

The big scribe nodded approvingly, smiled, and addressed the Great Intergalactic Council.

"Esteemed members of the Council, I respectfully ask that you cast your votes now. Who among you supports the preservation of the inhabitants of planet Ambassador in sector 54378-GT and the establishment of conditions conducive to successful symbiosis? Additionally, I urge you to vote in favor of removing the consciousness control device within the time loop!"

---

[3] *"Pulvis Iridis"* is a Latin phrase that translates to "powder of the rainbow" or "iris powder" in English.

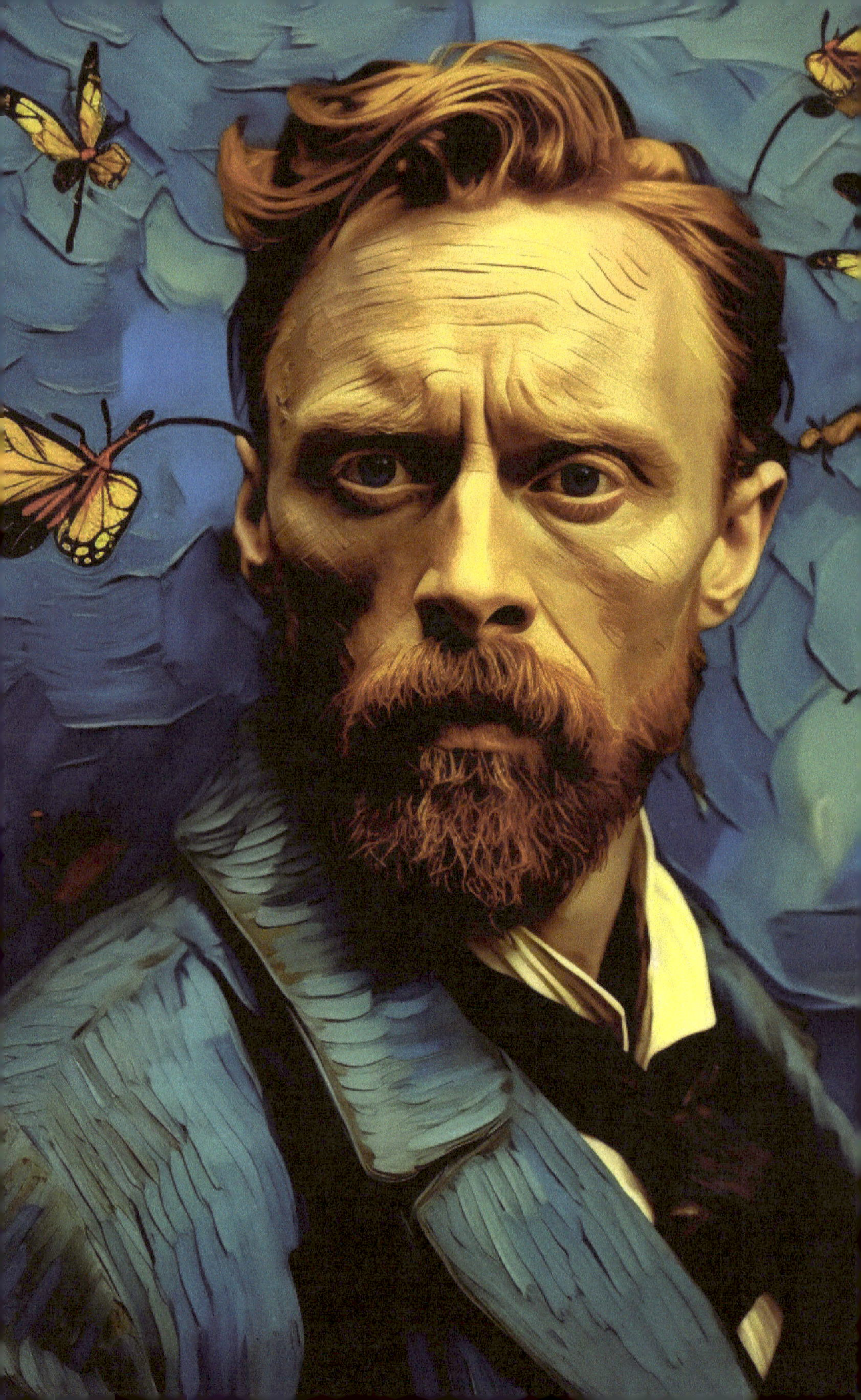

A few minutes later, the assistant scribe brought in the voting results, and the chief scribe announced them with a pleasant demeanor.

"The vote of the Great Intergalactic Council has officially concluded! By unanimous decision, the Council has approved the petition from planet Ambassador, endorsing the creation of conditions necessary for the successful symbiosis of its inhabitants, ensuring a long and fulfilling life. The Council has also decreed that the participating shmyg be returned to his natural habitat in the dungeons of planet Ambassador, where he, along with his kin, will undergo transformation into a new species, *Shmygus Humanus*. Furthermore, the consciousness control device within the time loop is to be dismantled, and all records of its existence shall be expunged."

Supreme Observer bowed to the Council. He straightened himself and settled the bright blue butterfly from his shoulder on his right index finger. He lifted his hand, and the butterfly freely waved its wings and flew toward the blue sky. The enormous toad-like creature clapped her front limbs together loudly. In horror, Baltz and Karl woke up and ran to their homes, screaming at the top of their lungs.

# Chapter 36

# The Diagnosis

*The lunatic, the lover, and the poet are of imagination all compact.*

*A Midsummer Night's Dream*, William Shakespeare

The Lecture of Professor Grayus Graf, "Cases of Mass Hallucinations and Their Scientific Explanation"

University of California School of Medicine, Los Angeles, Present day

Professor Grayus waited patiently for all the students to take a seat and began.

"In 1885, during the cholera epidemic, many villagers near Naples reported seeing the Madonna draped in black cloth, praying for the people at a chapel on a hill. The vision was so vivid that rumors of the incident began to spread throughout the district. To prevent unrest, the Italian government deployed the carabinieri to the hill, and this action alone helped to shield the people from the vision. As we now understand, the villagers neither witnessed a miracle nor experienced a collective moment of insanity. This incident has become one of the most famous examples of mass hallucination."

The lecturer paused, took out a pipe from his jacket pocket, and calmly took his first big puff. He held his breath a little and released a large tangle of toroidal smoke toward the audience. Students who had struggled to stay awake woke up instantly. A buzz of approval swept through the lecture hall as the students recognized the mild smell. The lecturer got comfortable in a chair by the table.

After making sure that all the attention of the students belonged to him, he continued, carelessly holding the pipe.

"Let's explore the concept of a hallucination. The *Oxford Guide to Psychiatry* provides a precise definition: 'A hallucination is a perceptual experience that occurs in the absence of an external stimulus to the sensory organs, yet is qualitatively similar to a real perception.' It is recognized by the individual as resembling an actual object in the external world and can be induced by various factors, including organic brain lesions, affective and dissociative disorders, and schizophrenia. Hallucinations can very rarely occur in healthy individuals, particularly in severe cases of being overworked, as well as during the processes of falling asleep or awakening."

The lecturer abruptly rose from his chair, pointing his pipe toward the audience.

"However, collective hallucinations are a completely different topic. Obviously, organic pathologies manifesting in the same manner in a group of people is impossible. It is also unlikely that all individuals who have experienced mass hallucinations suffer from schizophrenia. So, what are the objective reasons behind this phenomenon?"

He looked at the students with expectation, giving the audience a bit more time. Then, he took a deep puff, held his breath for a moment, and exhaled all the smoke through his nose. After a brief pause, he laughed loudly. His laughter, while inciting fear among the students, made them listen even more attentively.

"Well, the answer to this question lies on the surface."

The lecturer smiled widely.

"After all, the main factor is someone's willingness to believe not only their own eyes but also the eyes of another person—to be involved in someone's amazing imagination of something fantastic, fabulous, and incredible. As the psychologist D. Rockliff wrote: 'Where there is a faith in miracles, there will always be evidence of their existence. Faith produces hallucinations, and hallucinations confirm its conviction.'"

# Chapter 37

# The Hospital

*Everything we see hides another thing; we always want to see what is hidden by what we see.*

René Magritte

Stewart and Lynda Resnick Neuropsychiatric Hospital, University of California, Los Angeles, Present day

"Give me my butterfly!" a patient said to a nurse. "I saw you catch the butterfly and hide her in your pocket."

The nurse looked at him kindly and replied politely, "My dear Lucius, here she is. I just caught her for you."

She smiled and offered him her palm with an imaginary butterfly on it. "My butterfly!" he exclaimed. He joyfully grabbed his imaginary butterfly and rushed over to join the other patients in the room, who were quietly engaged in activities.

In this large room designed for relaxation and communication, everyone smiled and conversed. However, most engaged in conversations with imaginary interlocutors. Two people sat next to each other and did not smile at all. One appeared to be in his late fifties, while the other was a young man. The door to the room opened, and two people walked in, dressed in white coats like medical doctors. One of them acted as a guide, showing the other man around the hospital.

"Here, we have a lounge for patients experiencing persistent hallucinations," he said quietly to his companion.

"This is our kindest Maria, our fairy and nurse in one person."

He pointed at the nurse while saying hello to her. She nodded in response, and her cheeks got a bit pink.

"Maria, this is Professor Grayus Graff from the University of Munich. He traveled here all the way from Germany. The professor specializes in mass hallucinations and comes to us directly from the lecture he gave today to the medical students at our university."

Professor Grayus respectfully bowed his head and greeted Maria. Her cheeks got even more pink. The professor smiled, amused at the embarrassment of the junior medical staff.

"Here are the two patients you were interested in visiting today." He pointed at the silent, gritty pair.

"They are not verbose. One of them speaks only Italian, and the other speaks only French. They have tried to talk to each other, unsuccessfully, of course. They do not understand each other at all."

The doctor giggled in a barely noticeable manner and continued.

"It certainly looks like they know each other very well. We have learned some information from their stories. They claimed to have lived in the century before the last one, in some town called Grayville. They worked together at the railway. The older man said his name was Baltz. He allegedly worked as a steam locomotive engineer. The second one said his name was Karl. He used to work as his assistant. Honestly, there is little to nothing that surprises me these days," he said confidently.

"In twenty years of work, I have heard thousands of incredible stories. But they talked about some sort of intergalactic council and some kind of guardians. Most importantly, their stories are absolutely identical. Actually, their way of describing everything in the story, for a moment, made it sound plausible to me. Hhmm..."

The doctor patiently looked at the professor as if expecting a helpful response.

The professor respectfully smiled at his colleague. After taking a short pause to consider everything he had heard, Grayus spoke with a smile.

"I understand you, Doctor. I have been involved in the scientific research and explanation of collective hallucinations over the past ten years. This case is very interesting and sounds out of the ordinary. You probably know Professor Marco Iacoboni—who, by the way, is a neurologist and researcher at UCLA. His theory of mirror neurons explains a lot. The defects of the mirror neuron system can underlie various mental disorders.

"Let's assume that among these individuals, one is in perfect health and the other has a mental illness. During their interaction, they engage in what can be described as mirror-neuronal contact, where the dysfunctional neurons of the mentally ill person are reflected in the brain of the healthy individual. The fact is, now the healthy person experiences emotions identical to the mentally ill person."

The professor reached for his pipe, then remembered that smoking was prohibited in the hospital.

"I know quite a few languages. Will you let me talk to them?" He asked the doctor with a curious smile.

The doctor nodded, and the professor approached the two silent men. He smiled and looked at them kindly, thinking about what exactly to say to them. Then, he quickly began to speak Italian and French, addressing the first and the second patient. The two men enthusiastically communicated with the professor. At the end of the conversation, they joyfully hugged him and sat down. Now, they looked absolutely happy.

Professor Grayus approached the doctor, who regarded him with the admiration of a student looking up to a teacher.

"This is unbelievable! Dear Professor, how did you manage this? What did you say to them?" He asked, barely restraining his curiosity.

The professor smiled at him.

"I've said that I believed them. I also advised them to stick to the medical plan, assuring them that they will both improve and become absolutely healthy very soon. Excuse me, Doctor, I must leave now. Please, there's no need to escort me."

He shook hands with the doctor and quickly exited the room, closing the door behind him.

The doctor was so delighted by his experience with the professor that he did not notice when Maria approached him from behind and pulled his sleeve.

Surprised, the doctor jumped up slightly, turned to her, and addressed her irritably.

"Maria, I've told you before not to sneak up on me like that!"

"I am sorry! I didn't mean to scare you, Doctor. I've overheard your conversation with the professor."

She began to speak almost in a whisper as if she had just learned some terrible secret.

"In my youth, I lived in Naples for a long time. I know Italian very well."

Curious, the doctor gazed at her as she proceeded with her explanation.

"The professor didn't tell you the truth. Instead of addressing the topic you mentioned, he inquired about the location of planet Galanthus and then promised that he could bring them back home today, provided they recounted everything they experienced there. He disclosed that his son had recently completed a device capable of time travel and memory modification, assuring them there was no cause for concern. Furthermore, he offered to remove any troubling memories they possessed, guaranteeing they could proceed with their lives as if those events had never transpired."

The doctor was surprised by her side of the story. He looked at Maria and could not believe his ears. She continued to reveal more of the story.

"They shared with him everything he wanted to know. Subsequently, he assured them they would be home in a few minutes, just as he had promised. He emphasized that it was crucial for them to remain in their places."

They turned to look at the chairs where Baltz and Karl had been sitting just a couple of minutes ago, only to find them empty.

# Chapter 38

# The Insight

*Insight encompasses the capacity to achieve profound and intuitive comprehension of a person, situation, or concept. It entails discerning and grasping the true essence or underlying mechanisms of something, frequently with sudden clarity. Insight usually emerges from a blend of observation, reflection, and intuition, culminating in a deeper understanding or revelation. It can be attained through personal experiences, introspection, or the counsel of others.*

*The Greatest Largest Shmygopedia*

Grayus sat in his office, enveloped in silence. At last, all the pieces of the puzzle that had tormented him throughout his life clicked into place in his mind. Despite feeling indignant upon discovering that his entire species existed solely because a certain chief agrobiologist had failed to fulfill his duties properly, he also felt a sense of gratitude. Were it not for this oversight, the shmygs would not exist—nor would the magical plant.

He was aware of the sanctions and authorizations allowing all shmygs to transition into another species, termed "humane shmygs." Soon, all manipulations would be aimed exclusively at benefiting the human-dolls.

In the history of the shmygs, the civilization of human-dolls had been annihilated at least twice. Shmyg scientists had never been able to explain this phenomenon or comprehend how the human-dolls managed to resurrect themselves and repopulate the planet fully. Now, everything made perfect sense.

However, numerous questions still lingered in his mind. Why is it necessary to raise human-dolls as if they were plants in a garden? What is the purpose of this garden called Earth? Why is this world isolated from other worlds, including the community that had created it? Why are shmygs given the abhorrent name of *Shmygus Infestantibus*? Who invented all of this, and why?

He took a deep puff from his pipe. The questions took shape and flew around his head like satellites flying around the orbit of their planet. After a second, more deliberate puff, he paused longer before letting the smoke drift out through his nostrils. Laughing heartily, he imagined the planet morphing into a rocket, breaking free from the orbit of these nagging satellites of inquiry. In this escape, both the planet and his mind found liberation from their relentless chase.

He picked up the key he had found at the Antiqua Bibliotheca and carefully examined it. The book he had found there did not provide any answers, but it hinted at the direction he should take. He spun the key in his hands. On one side, a barely visible arrow flashed, pointing from the head of the key to its tip. He turned the key again, and the arrow briefly reappeared before vanishing.

He moved his thumb along the key in the direction the arrow had pointed. Suddenly, a portal appeared in the middle of the office, and a man with red hair, mustache, and beard emerged. In comparison with Grayus, he seemed a giant, but he did not invoke fear. He smiled good-naturedly at Grayus as he approached the small, stressed shmyg and extended his hand for a handshake. Slightly embarrassed, Grayus shook the stranger's hand.

After a short pause, the man introduced himself.

"You can call me the Artist. I have been looking after this world for a very, very long time. One might even say I created it."

He took an ancient photo card out of his pocket and handed it over to Grayus. Grayus looked at the photo and saw the man sitting on his haunches, smiling. Around him, humans and shmygs, the latter resembling children, were gathered closely. Grayus returned the photograph, and the man continued his story.

"I knew then that the chief agrobiologist had made a mistake. Well, personally, I didn't consider it a mistake. I saved your kind during the first sweep, but I couldn't save the humans. At the time, I couldn't explain to all of you why the sweep had happened. I knew your great-great-great-grandfather very well—I was very close friends with him. This key is a replica of the key I gave to him in the hope that one day, everything would change, and you would again live on the surface of the planet at peace with yourselves and with all the humans. Now, the time has come."

Grayus looked at him incredulously and spoke with sorrow. "Still, after all, they have decided to transform us into a different species."

The Artist laughed loudly.

"This is just a well-forgotten "old" kind of your species. In that photo, you have just seen the species you'll transition to in due course. Trust me. You're going to love living on the surface of the Earth. See the visible, know the well-known, open the unlocked."

He looked at Grayus with the affection a father might show his son, then pulled a pipe from his pocket and handed it over. Grayus took the deepest puff of his life, holding his breath for as long as possible. When he exhaled, multicolored smoke clouds in various shapes billowed out, forming rainbows. Suddenly, the questions that had tormented Grayus found their answers, and he understood the creation of the universe.

# Chapter 39

# The Rainbow

*Every soul crafts its own spectrum of rainbows; let the colors flow without bounds. The souls deeply acquainted with the essence of joy dance in rhythm with the ebb and flow of existence, delighting in the ephemeral beauty of soap bubbles that catch the sun's embrace, weaving tiny rainbows. These souls are the true connoisseurs of happiness.*

The Artist's Personal Journal

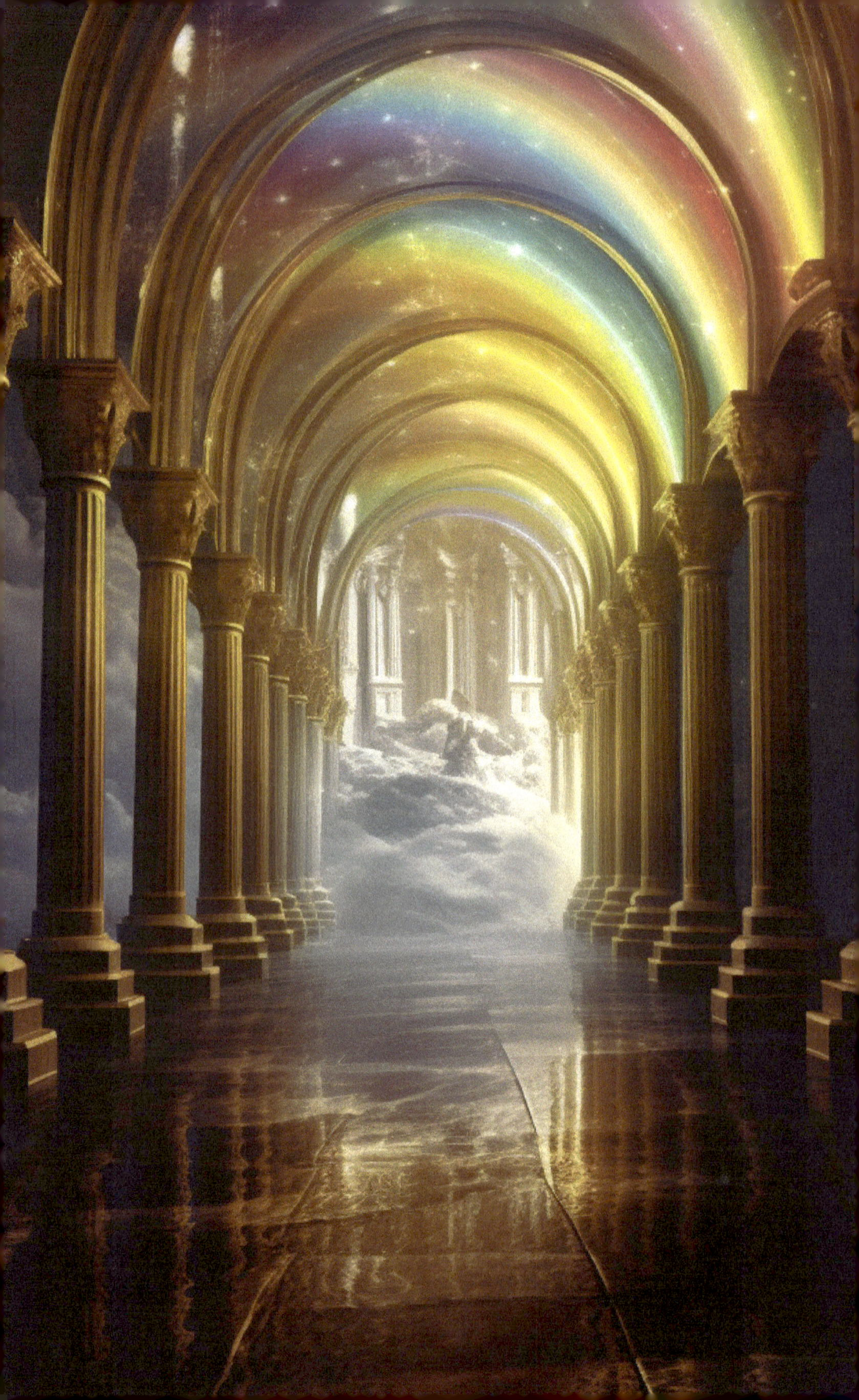

The Artist sat on a chair beside a canvas filled with gray sketches, his smile radiating quiet satisfaction. Light poured into the vast hall, illuminating gold columns and revealing walls adorned with countless paintings, each depicting different worlds. With a casual wave of his brush, a stream of light exploded into multicolored brilliance, as if showered with gemstones glinting in the sunlight. He guided the brush through this luminous cascade, then brought it to the canvas. Suddenly, the brush came to life. On its own, it created atop the canvas a fantastical rainbow, embracing every color known to the human world.

# Chapter 40

# The Pollination

*Happiness is not something ready-made. It comes from your own actions.*

Dalai Lama

Intergalactic Spacecraft Carrier, UMION, Class Alpha

Sector 54378-GT, somewhere above the trial planet Ambassador, a.k.a. Earth

The chief agrobiologist's enormous module was filled with smoke. His hookah resembled a steam locomotive, emitting continuous puffs of smoke, while his favorite song played at full volume through the speakers. The friendly voice of the duty officer on the main bridge came through the communication speaker.

"Mr. Chief Agrobiologist, sir, we have stopped the core of the planet. Now, we are fully ready to go ahead with the rainbow dust pollination procedure. We are awaiting your instructions."

The turtle-looking being coughed after a strong puff and momentarily addressed the duty officer in a strict voice.

"Officer, I kindly request that you verify once more to ensure the planet's core has been completely immobilized. It must be entirely devoid of any movement, however slight. Failing to do so risks a repeat of the catastrophe we witnessed on planet Dushont, which ultimately was left with nothing but asteroids. There's a significant difference between pollinating a planet and having to recreate it and its inhabitants from scratch. Unless, of course, you're prepared to be stationed here for thirty moons."

From the hesitation at the other end of the line, it was clear that the officer was in doubt. After a few seconds, he replied in a friendly manner.

"Yes, sir! Definitely! I will double-check. I don't want to be stuck here for thirty moons. My brother-in-law's wedding is in fourteen moons, and I don't want to miss it for anything. His bride makes the best leech cider in all of Krishane."

"Congratulations! I am very happy for you, Lieutenant!" said the chief agrobiologist. After a moment, he added, "I would gladly join you if it

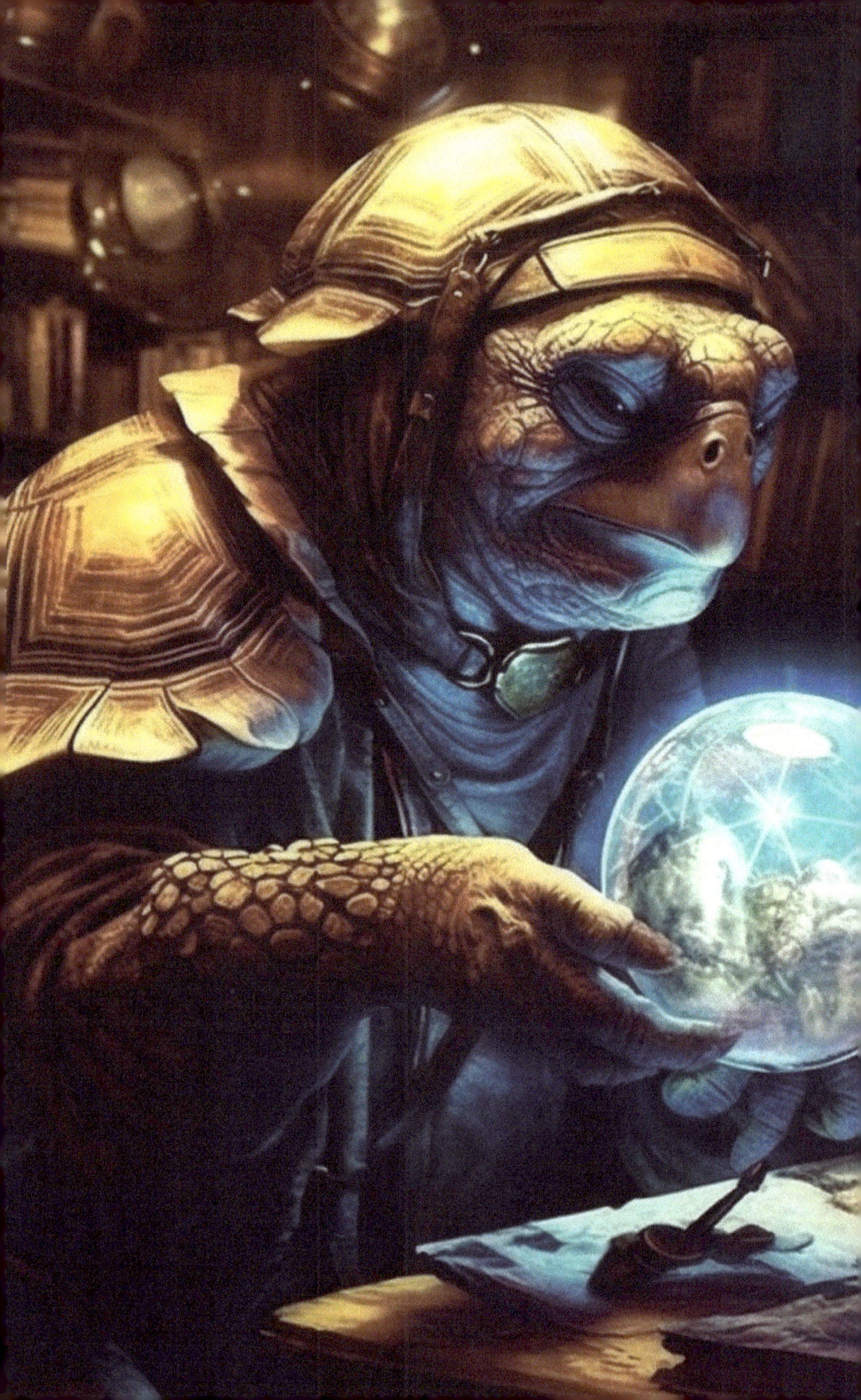

weren't for my congenital allergy to leeches. I am awaiting your report confirming full readiness."

"Of course, sir! I apologize; I will report in a couple of minutes!" the duty officer responded in a more serious tone of voice.

Suddenly, the connection was severed, and the song resumed playing. The being ascended to the massive computer on the platform, initiating the required modifications to the DNA and RNA sequences of all living organisms. This process was meticulously synchronized with the active *Pulvis Iridis* particles.

The duty officer's voice rang out from the speaker once more. "Sir, full readiness has been confirmed. We had to accelerate time on the planet a few times over. You were right. At the time of my first report, there was a slight inertial movement inside the core of the planet. I have the signed procedural documents here from the chief engineer in my hands."

"Start pulverizing the synchronized *Pulvis Iridis* compound!" the chief agrobiologist replied calmly. After a few moments, he added, "I will handle everything else myself!"

"Acknowledged!" reported the duty officer from the main bridge. Then, he disconnected.

With a mere thought, the chief agrobiologist projected an image of the planet into the center of the module and monitored the procedure intently.

Initially, he was concerned that the compound was being distributed unevenly. However, it appeared that the chief engineer had fine-tuned the dispersal rate, thereby stabilizing Earth's atmosphere.

Once the pulverization procedure was complete, the chief agrobiologist accelerated time on the planet several times over, observing the atmospheric changes in "real-time." After these changes ceased, he displayed all current indicators beside the planet's image. Having carefully studied the readings, he began to speak. "Lieutenant, the atmosphere has stabilized! Dispatch seven gas transporters. We need to adjust the ratio of nitrogen to oxygen; otherwise, given the current state of affairs, all life will be devoid of an atmosphere within sixty moons. I will send you precise data, including coordinates and necessary volumes of all gasses."

"Clear, sir! The gas transporters have been deployed. Three, two, one... pumping has commenced," the lieutenant concluded his report. After a brief pause, he added, "Sir, may I discuss a personal matter with you?"

The turtle-looking being took a deep puff and exhaled, forming the shape of a UMION spacecraft carrier with the smoke, then answered, "Of course, you may, Lieutenant! We have a couple of minutes until the balancing of gasses is complete."

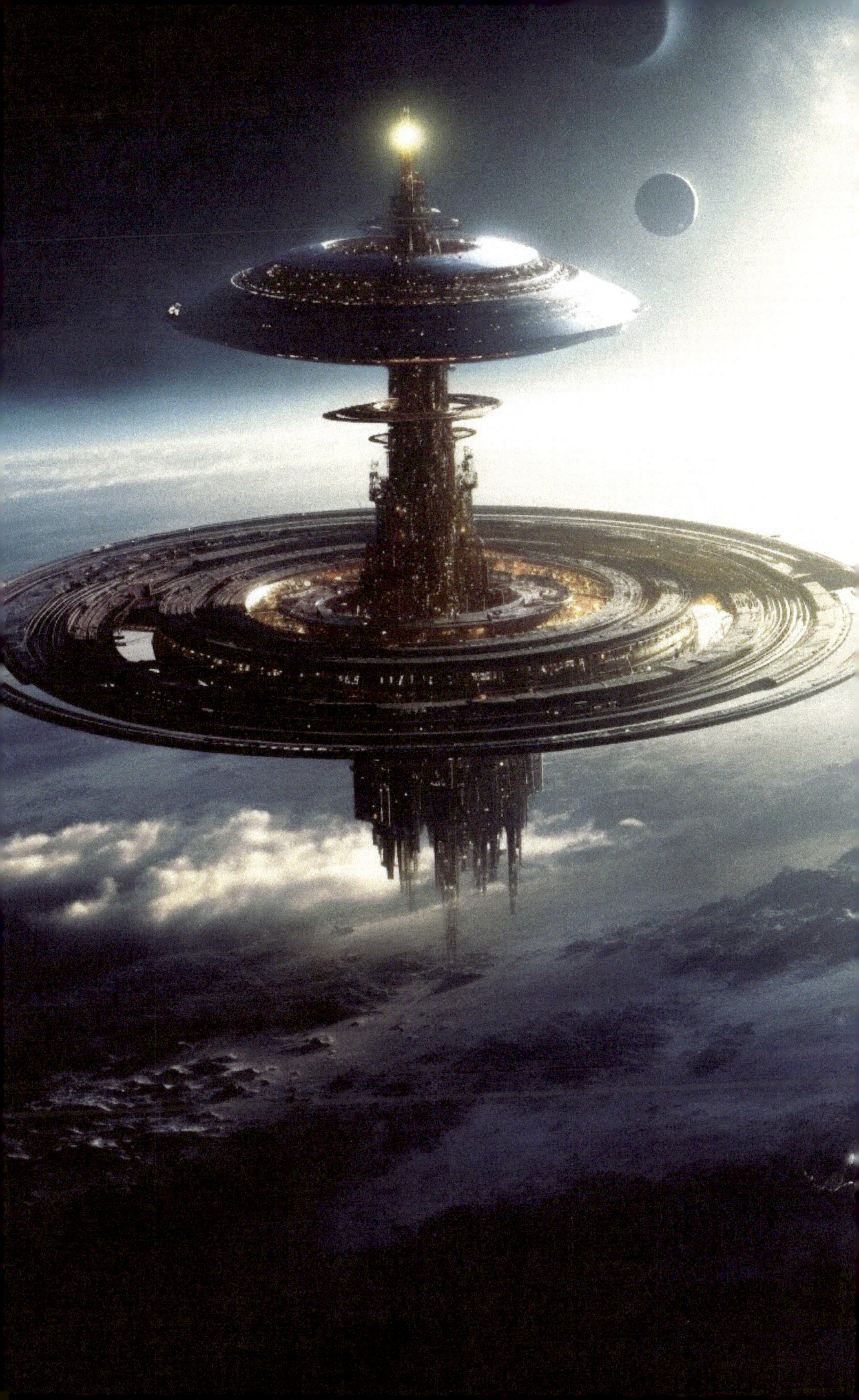

"Sir, don't you feel sorry for all the inhabitants living on the trial planets?" the duty officer asked with a hint of sadness in his voice.

It seemed the chief agrobiologist was a bit shocked by this question, and after a few seconds, he kindly replied.

"Son, you must understand that all trial planets are essentially prisons. The inhabitants there have all committed serious offenses. Their entire world is an illusion. We hope that, upon completing this operation, we will significantly improve the lives of those on planet Ambassador. I wish for them to live in harmony with the entire universe. Remember, the trial planets were established to encourage the inhabitants to learn from their mistakes and offer them an opportunity for continued evolution. Incidentally, my own brother is serving time on planet Ambassador for his involvement in the Kvazarian catastrophe."

"Was he the one who killed the entire crew and all the passengers on that shuttle during an emergency landing?" asked the duty officer with surprise.

"Yes, that was him. The fool fell asleep right at the helm, and the autopilot failed. Anyway, don't trouble your mind with this nonsense; you're still young! When you've exchanged the first hundred thousand years for some experience, your perspective will shift. I'm just a couple of cycles away from retirement. Once I receive approval from the Supreme Celestial, I plan to leave it all behind and spend my days in the ocean with the wild turtles, perhaps even on this planet." he replied, his voice filled with joyful anticipation.

"Sir, I envy you, but in the best way possible! However, as a being from the macaque family, my idea of happiness is somewhat different." The lieutenant cheerfully continued, "There's nowhere I'd rather be than in a thicket of wild palm trees, jumping around and feasting on fresh bananas."

"Don't worry, Lieutenant! Eventually, you'll reach your retirement too," the chief agrobiologist responded. "And then, all the bananas from Dushont Palm Park will be yours for the taking."

"Last season, my family and I visited Dushont Palm Park. We encountered more elephants, crocodiles, and wild pigs than we could count. I still have a vivid memory of one particularly plump hippopotamus," the duty officer replied jokingly.

The chief agrobiologist laughed loudly for a moment, then said, "Come on, Lieutenant! Just so you know, that 'fat hippo' is the first chief architect and one of the creators of our home, planet Galanthus."

Suddenly, their conversation was interrupted by the voice of the chief engineer coming through the communication speaker.

"Sir, the process of balancing the gasses is complete. I have just updated all the indicators for you. Please take a look."

The chief agrobiologist glanced at the image of the planet and the updated indicators next to it, then announced with a happy smile.

"Congratulations, my dear colleagues! Operation *Pulvis Iridis* has been successfully completed! I thank you all for your exceptional work. Now, it's time for us to return home."

# Chapter 41

# What A Wonderful World

*And forget not that the earth delights to feel your bare feet and the winds long to play with your hair.*

Khalil Gibran, *The Prophet*

It was noon, and elder statesman Sippley was walking around Grayville, an activity that was peculiar and never part of his daily routine. Typically, at this time, having completed most of the town's duties, he would return home to his wife, Rickma. Together, they would share a meal, after which he would promptly return to his desk to resume his duties as the town's elder statesman.

At this moment, however, much to his surprise, while he enjoyed a leisurely stroll, he felt a highly unusual lightness of the mind. He felt as if the whole mountain had been pressing upon him all this time and now it was lifted.

As he moved away from the church building and made his way down through Gray Street, it was as though he was rediscovering Grayville anew. He paused, taking in his surroundings. Suddenly, a wave of sadness overcame him. The pervasive grayness of the town stirred a sense of discomfort within him, plunging him into a state of emptiness, meaninglessness, and confusion.

He continued his walk, hoping this condition would leave him. As he approached Black Lane, he noticed a new house, but his attention was quickly drawn to a huge black cat sitting on a bench outside the house. The cat wore a white shirt with a black tuxedo, white shoes with black toes, and a black top hat. The cat sat in a pose like people do with their legs crossed, with one paw over the other. He swayed his paws up and down and seemed relaxed, enjoying the day. When he saw Sippley walking over to him, he took out a golden pince-nez and placed it on his nose. Then, he pulled a golden pocket watch from his pocket, checked the time, and spoke politely,

"The honorable Sippley Andris! I am very pleased to finally make your acquaintance. Basil, Doctor of Philosophy, at your service!"

To his surprise, Sippley felt at ease; he was not at all astonished to see the talking cat in front of him.

Though not fully understanding what was happening, Sippley continued the conversation.

"May I ask, how do you know my name?"

"Oh, I've heard a lot about the elder statesman of Grayville, the most respected Sippley Andris. Amazingly, you manage to keep the whole town running on time, with the precision of a clock's hands. This is indeed an invaluable talent! How did you manage it? Moore-meow," Basil asked with a smile.

"I am just an ordinary person who serves the town," replied Sippley modestly.

"Well, my kind friend, you are very special! There's a lot more to you than you think. Would you like to find out for yourself, moore-meow?" The cat moved a little and winked.

Sippley's heart had never been filled with such delight and joy, emotions he had lacked his whole life. Eager to pursue these feelings further, he replied with sincerity, "With great pleasure, dear Doctor!"

The cat clicked his paws, and the door to the new house opened. He pointed to the entrance and said invitingly, "Please, dear, come in!"

Sippley went inside, and the door closed behind him. He suddenly found himself in Grayville again. However, it was not the town he had known. This was like a new and improved Grayville. It was a bit larger and filled with colors. All the houses were brightly painted and had gardens filled with colorful flowers. Bright green trees grew everywhere. Sippley walked down Gray Street, which had lost its gray color completely. A beautiful fountain in the shape of a fisherman holding a large golden fish stood in all its glory right in the center of the town near the blue church building. Sippley stood there, stunned.

Suddenly, he heard a kind, pleasant inner voice saying, "Sippley, do not be shy! This is a part of your beautiful creation! Take a walk and see how talented you are!"

In all his sixty-three years, Sippley could not recall a time he felt more delighted than in this moment. He embarked on the same walk he had taken earlier that day, but now, he genuinely desired to live in Grayville.

Sippley paused his walk for a moment, realizing that everything was about to change. He absorbed the festive and colorful atmosphere of the beautiful town, smiling to himself. Resuming his stroll, he approached the first bakery on Gray Street. To his surprise, he found Karl and Baltz sitting at a table outside. Each had colorful desserts on their beautiful plates, and they shared laughs while they sipped honey krupnik. An empty chair at their table caught his eye, amplifying his happiness—he was eager to join them and share his unbelievable story. Sitting down, he looked at them with a joyful smile.

Baltz was delighted that Sippley had joined their table. He had missed his good friend and was eager to share the beautiful aromas of his freshly made, new and improved batch of krupnik.

"Sippley, is that really you? What joy that of all people, you're the first to join us today! Karl and I were just speaking of you. Remember, Karl? We mentioned how wonderful it would be to sip krupnik together with our friend Sippley. Would you like some? I've just made a new batch, which Karl and I have been enjoying this afternoon."

"It would be my honor to join you and taste your magical drink!"

Sippley replied happily.

Baltz took another glass from the inner pocket of his jacket, placed it in front of Sippley, and poured a bright, amber liquid into it that shimmered in the sunlight. Then, he filled the glasses to the top for Karl and himself.

All three took the glasses in their hands, and Karl made a toast.

"Welcome to the new Grayville! To this wonderful feeling of lightness, openness, freedom, joy, and happiness!"

As they drank, their eyes happened to turn upward, and they saw a beautiful, outlandish rainbow with all known colors. The rainbow sparkled everywhere as if it were strewn with precious stones.

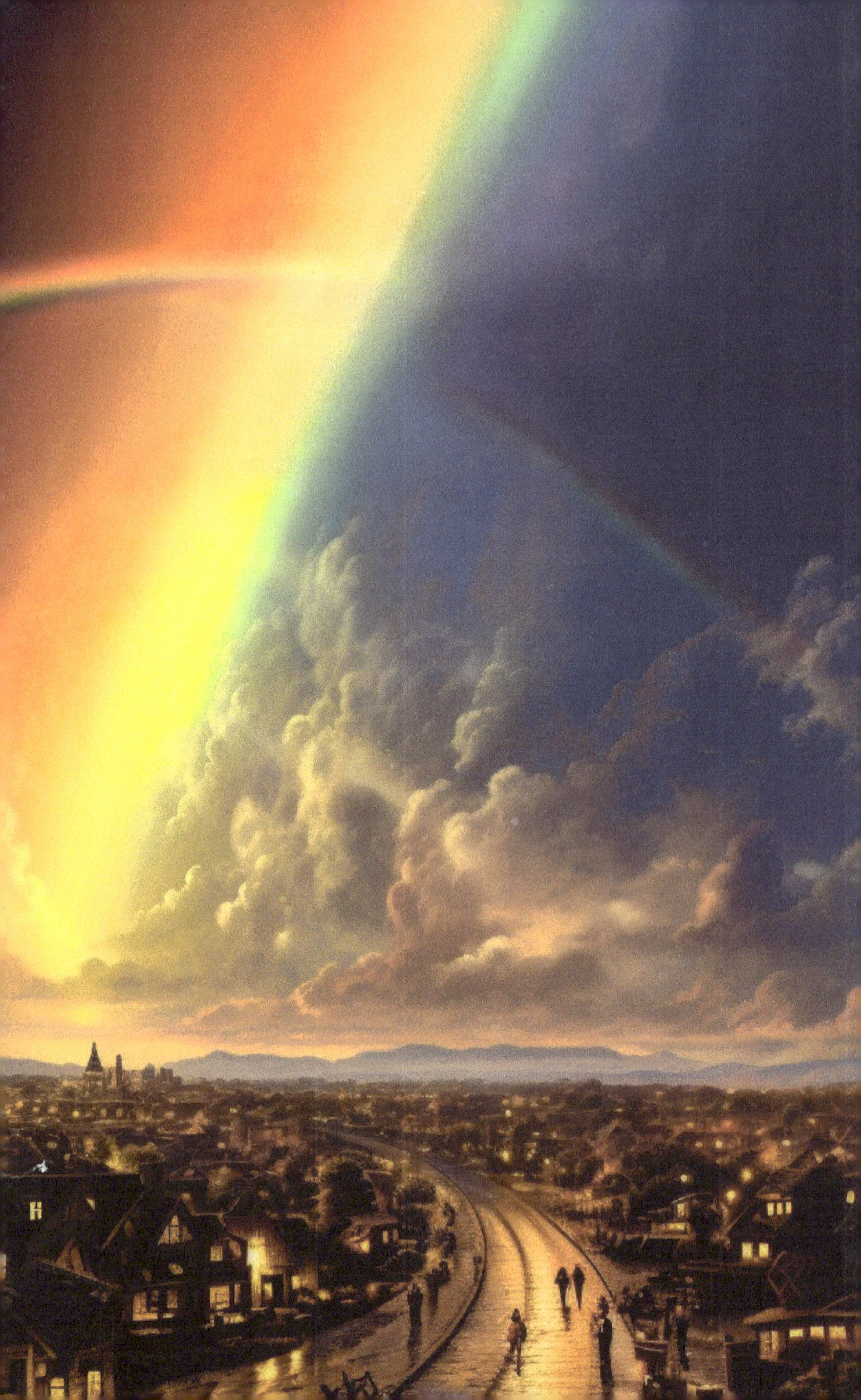

After precisely seven minutes to the second, all the residents of Grayville gathered at the main square by the fountain. They had left their homes after they saw the unusually beautiful, glittering rainbow outside their windows. The rainbow was huge—so wide and big that it seemed it could cover the Earth all around.

It sank slowly. Everyone looked right up at it, enchanted and unable to take their eyes off it. They had the feeling that it would envelop the whole planet. When the rainbow light overtook Grayville, all its inhabitants basked in euphoria. Everybody felt incredible lightness, freedom, openness, and—most importantly—sincere happiness. All the townspeople had tears of joy in their eyes because they were looking at each other for the first time.

They rejoiced and hugged each other. Some people danced happily together to the most beautiful music, which was flowing from somewhere in the sky. Everyone was so overwhelmed with sincere feelings of happiness and love that they failed to notice the captivating, sparkling rainbow descending into the ground.

"Also, cheers to the honor and respect of our old friend, the big man, krupnik! Hear, hear!" added Baltz with joyful pride.

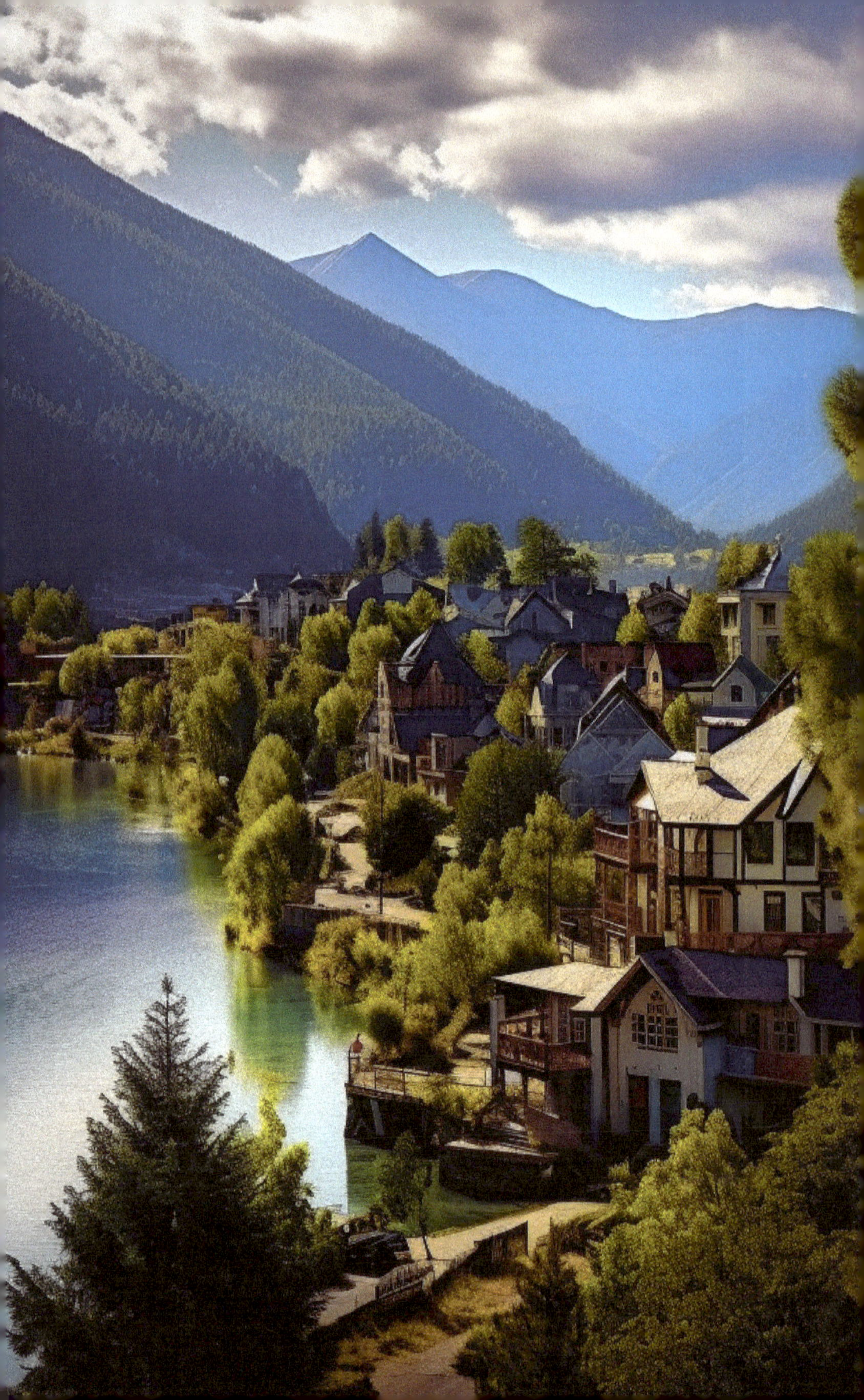

Suddenly, beautiful rainbow bubbles began to descend from the sky, landing on people's heads. After the rain of rainbow bubbles ended, every single person on Earth heard a kind, inner voice speaking to them.

"Now, you are free to do as you please! We love you and wish you kindness. You have been liberated and your free will, along with your talents, has been restored. Cherish this gift, nurture it, and understand that your talents can only be utilized through the goodwill of your hearts. Love one another and sincerely wish each other well—you all are one big family! Protect this beautiful planet; it is your only home!"

# Chapter 42

# Sky

*The highest knowledge is to know that we are surrounded by mystery. Neither knowledge nor hope for the future can be the pivot of our life or determine its direction. It is intended to be solely determined by our allowing ourselves to be gripped by the ethical God, who reveals Himself in us, and by yielding our will to His.*

Albert Schweitzer

Heavenly abode, Ghost planet
Unknown time and place

After successfully completing the mission on planet Ambassador, the Supreme Celestial aimed to personally deliver his sincere and profound gratitude to Lea, the chief guardian. Stepping out of the portal, Lea landed on a floor barely visible to the eye. As transparent as glass, it appeared to hover in midair, seemingly supported by nothing. Clouds were everywhere, interspersed with bright celestial light. A boundless alley of bizarrely huge trees stretched before her, leading to massive gates in the distance.

No one she knew had ever been invited to an audience with the Supreme Celestial. No one had ever ventured here before, and no one had ever conveyed how incredibly beautiful it was. At a leisurely pace, she moved toward the enormous golden gates, all the while attentively observing everything around her. Various peculiar animals, each equipped with wings, hopped about in the trees. Many different birds of unprecedented beauty sang everywhere, and charming, fluffy hedgehogs scurried underfoot.

One of them ran straight up to her and poked her directly in the leg with his nose. She picked him up and brought him to her face. He looked at her closely with cute, narrow eyes and seemed to smile. Then suddenly, he licked her nose, wriggled free from her hands, nimbly jumped down, and immediately hid in the foliage of the nearest shrub. She continued on her way, trying to remember as many details as possible in order to describe all this incredible beauty to her friends.

It seemed that she had been walking for several hours before she approached the gates. As soon as she touched them, a huge horn sounded from above, and two five-meter-tall angels almost instantly jumped down and blocked her path.

"Lea! He is waiting for you!" one of the angels proclaimed in a loud, booming voice, and with a sweep of his wing, he opened the gate.

"Enter, and do not deviate from your path!" He returned his wing to its place.

He then shook his head slightly, like a giant sparrow, and stood at the gate, sheathing his huge golden sword.

She stepped inside unhurriedly and saw a garden of indescribable splendor, with creatures even more incredible and stunning than those outside. There were simply no words in her vocabulary to describe all this magnificence. Everything here was perfect and harmonious. She moved slowly along the path, unable to take her eyes off one creature after another.

Giant fruits hung down from the branches of gigantic trees, the fragrances of heavenly beautiful flowers were everywhere, and pleasant music could be heard from a gazebo visible at the end of the path. The closer she got, the more clearly she could hear the melody. It seemed to her that she had known this melody since childhood.

In the gazebo sat an elderly man, bearded and clad completely in opulent white. He bore a striking resemblance to her idea of an ancient sage. His eyebrows were so lengthy that they mingled with His beard and mustache. As He played His flute, the music seemed to permeate her being, touching the most delicate strings of her soul. Suddenly, she realized that she had heard this melody at the moment of her birth. How long ago that was! It felt to her as if she had traversed an eternity. Unexpectedly, the melody faded, and the elderly man turned toward her. His face radiated absolute kindness, and His insightful gaze seemed to read all her thoughts.

"Lea, my dear girl! You remember this melody!" He exclaimed to her with a kind smile. "I played it for you at your birth to ease the pain of the transition to the Lower World. Please, sit beside me; I have something important to tell you."

Overwhelmed, she sat down, her thoughts scattered. Noticing her confusion, He offered a warm smile and continued.

"Long ago, you were an angel. You were among the most beautiful, strongest, and most perfect of my angels. I remember how your wings shone in bright golden hues, bathed in heavenly light. I remember the first time I showed you the Lower World; you wept at the sight of all the pain and suffering that filled it. You once asked me, 'Why is there so much pain and suffering?' To which I replied: 'Only by experiencing pain and suffering can one truly comprehend LOVE.' What is considered commonplace here in Heaven is inaccessible in the Lower World. However, only by breaking through the darkness can one find light."

"But how long will the suffering of the Lower World continue?" she suddenly asked with a tingle of bitterness in her heart.

The elderly man looked at her intently, then pulled a glowing orb out of His pocket, smiled, and replied.

"Until this orb is filled with light!" He held it up, and she saw that the orb was two-thirds full.

"When the last lost soul finds the light, thereby filling the orb, the Lower World will close forever at that very instant, putting an end to the perpetual cycle of suffering and pain. All who have found the light will remain in Heaven eternally, and those lost in the darkness will fade into oblivion."

Lea was sitting next to the elder, afraid to even move.

"But what about me? Why was I dispatched to the Lower World?" she suddenly asked.

He glanced at Lea kindly and replied with a faint smile.

"Your heart has always been brimming with compassion! You've constantly desired to assist others, alleviate their suffering, and help them discover the light! You volunteered to venture into the Lower World in hopes of saving as many lost souls as you could! And you're succeeding remarkably! Recently, you saved an entire planet! I've been diligently observing your achievements!" He smiled happily and patted her on the shoulder.

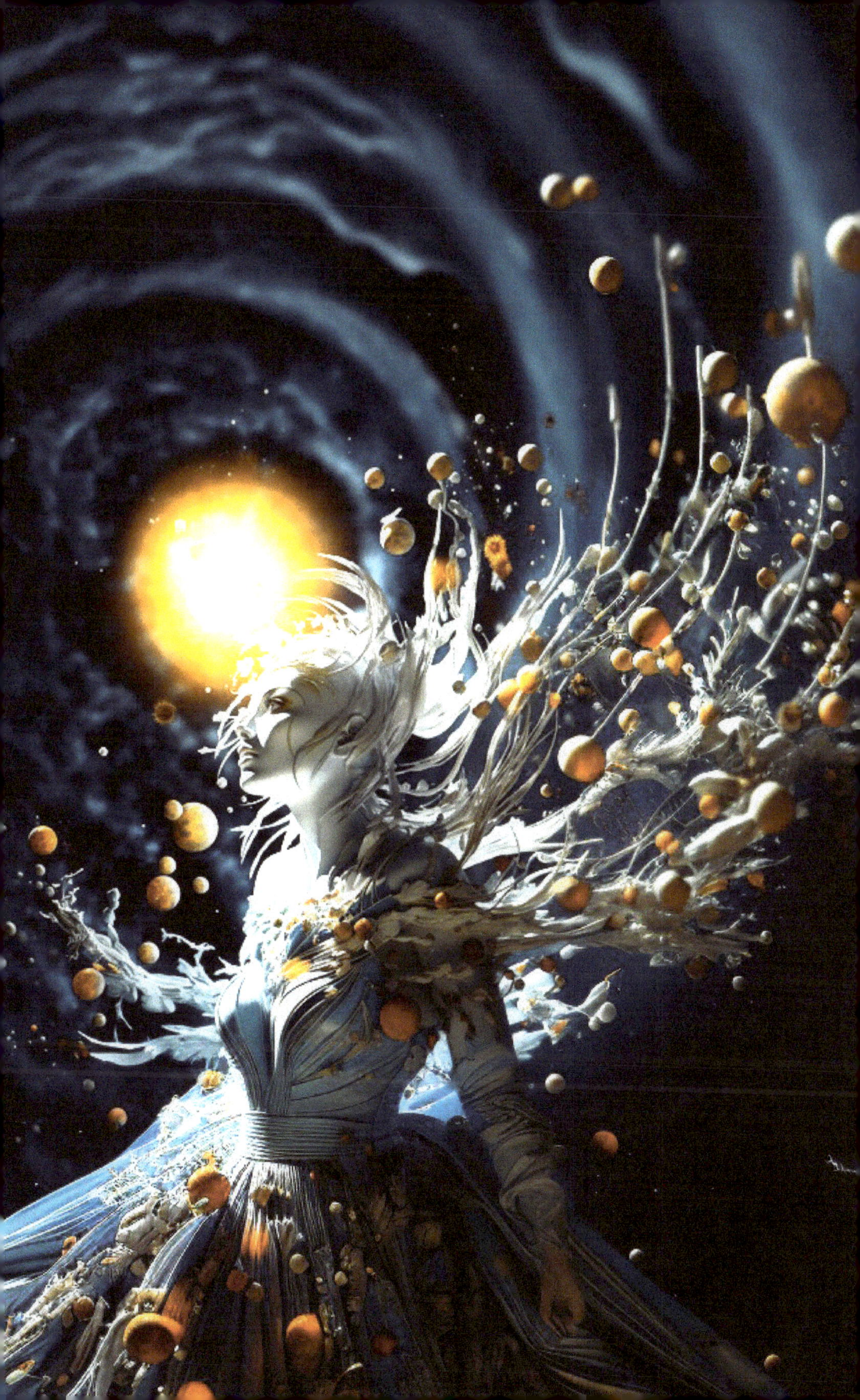

"Well, now you are faced with a choice once again: to stay here eternally or to continue your quest in the Lower World!"

"It sounds tempting to stay here in Heaven!" she replied cheerfully. "However, the orb is far from being full! There's still time to help others; it's too early to slack off!"

The elderly man laughed heartily and lightly patted her on the shoulder again.

"I knew you would respond like that!"

He whistled enthusiastically, and one of the fluffy hedgehogs came rushing over to him. He took the little fellow in his hands and gave it a slight smile, petted its little head, and handed the cutie to Lea.

"Hold this little one for a while! I have something to do!"

She took the hedgehog in her hands, and it seemed to her that it was the same little one from the alley that had licked her nose and then nimbly run away. She smiled, looking straight into its cunning eyes, and it seemed to smile back at her.

Suddenly, it licked her nose again, then many more times. The small hedgehog started to lick her face quickly, and squinting from the tickling, she began to giggle, afraid of dropping the little one from her hands. She laughed and kept saying out loud to her new friend to stop the licking. "Stop it, baby! It's so ticklish!... I'm ticklish!... Ticklish!..."

She suddenly jolted awake in her module aboard the Stellar Sentinel spacecraft, *Synus*. A huge artificial tongue immediately retreated into the doorway as *Synus* laughed loudly.

"How do you like my invention!? I named it a dog-licker! Now I'm going to wake all the crew members with this huge slippery tongue."

"Yuck! That's disgusting!" she replied, wrinkling her nose and wiping the sticky substance from her face.

*Synus* laughed again.

"Well, judging by how you called me 'baby' and giggled sweetly, you weren't that disgusted! But that's nothing. When I woke Leon up today, he stuck out his tongue, trying to kiss me passionately. When he realized that I was joking, he ran to the power block like a madman, trying to disconnect me from the power supply. But you know that it's impossible, my dear!" He switched to a mockingly playful tone. "After all, I'm fueled only by your love!" Again, he laughed cheerfully. Leon's agitated voice came from the speaker.

"We have just received a direct order from the Supreme Celestial! We are flying to Kurkura Mountain, in the TRY-891138 sector, to save another planet from self-destruction."

"Understood, Leon! Crew, report readiness in three minutes."

Lea quickly gave the order and swiftly jumped into a protective suit, but something in her pocket prevented her from fastening it. She reached into it and pulled out a glowing orb, which was two-thirds full. Lea bowed to the painting of the Supreme Celestial and quickly ran out of the module. She embarked on this new adventure by simply pressing the teleportation button on her gold bracelet, vanishing from the passageway within a fraction of a second.

Dear Reader,

Thank you for dedicating your time to our book! We sincerely hope you enjoyed the journey.

Any similarities to real-life individuals, in descriptions or illustrations, are purely coincidental and unintentional.

We are currently working on our second book and hope it will create many joyous memories for you. Continue to radiate brilliance and inspire others with your fabulous presence!

Respectfully,
Victoria & Dennis

Printed in the USA
CPSIA information can be obtained
at www.ICGtesting.com
LVHW050116021124
795331LV00013B/143